ALSO BY TONY JORDAN

*The Train*
*Flying Blind*

# Follow Me
## and Other Stories

# FOLLOW ME

## AND OTHER STORIES

❦

Tony Jordan

*Victoria
Follow Me!!
Tony J*

SPY HILL
PUBLISHING

Spy Hill Publishing

© 2016 by Tony Jordan
All rights reserved. This book or any portion thereof may not be reproduced or used in any manner without the express written permission of the publisher except for the use of brief quotations in a book review.

First Edition

This is a work of fiction. Names, characters, places, and incidents either are the products of the author's imagination or are used in a fictitious manner. Any resemblance to actual persons, living or dead, or to actual events is purely coincidental.

Library of Congress Control Number: 2016914616
Spy Hill Publishing, Clinton, TN

ISBN-13: 0692770631
ISBN-10: 9780692770634

Book and cover design by Nathan Armistead
Printed in the United States of America

*To Miss Anne,*
*without whom not one of my words would be published*
*and without whom I would not be who I am*

# Acknowledgments

⚜

To all the southerners and Yankees who unknowingly helped me write these stories, and to Michele and Nathan Armistead for their invaluable assistance and support throughout the publication process.

# CONTENTS

Follow Me ............................................. 1
A Real First Captain and More ...................... 39
Between Heaven and Hell ........................... 49
A December Rain .................................... 89
Fairies in the Garden .............................. 125
A Council of Crows ................................ 139
The Face ........................................... 147

# PREFACE

⚜

FATHERS AND SONS; HEROES; FRIENDS; uncles, aunts, and nephews; colleagues joined by pain and loyalty; fairies and mortals; brothers, sisters, and mothers. These stories deal with relationships and values across a subculture known as the American South. They are of a time and place where magic can still happen—whether it is the magic of fairies, the magic of love, or the everyday magic of just trying to do the right thing.

Enjoy!

# Follow Me
## and Other Stories

# Follow Me

❦

*July 1959, Brookley Air Force Base, Mobile, Alabama*
THE BUS STOPPED AT THE entrance to the flight line, its way barred by a red-and-white barrier. The passenger in the front seat, an air force lieutenant, got down and showed his badge to the guard. "Boy Scouts to tour the flight line."

The guard looked at the badge, stepped back, saluted, and raised the barrier so the bus could proceed.

All flight lines look enormous, but since this one had runways that stretched out into Mobile Bay, it looked even bigger. It had to be big, for sitting on the line were some of the largest airplanes in the US Air Force inventory, the C-124 Globemasters.

"Look!" one of the Scouts yelled. "It's Old Shaky!"

"Yes!" cried another from the very rear seat. "But look down there. All the way down. It's a B-52 Stratofortress!"

All eyes shifted toward the sleek, swept-wing bomber at the end of the line of aircraft. The sight elicited a collective "wow!"

The bus stopped in front of one of the C-124s. The lieutenant got out and motioned for the others to follow. "Everybody, fall in here," he said, indicating a yellow line that was painted on the concrete.

"Fall in on me!" the patrol leader called, jumping to a spot on the yellow line closest to the airplane. Since he held Star Scout rank and his father was the scoutmaster, he was, naturally, the leader of Tomahawk patrol. No one seemed to mind, although most of the time the others paid little attention to his orders, choosing mostly to go their own ways. Today, though, they were all on their best behavior, and each of the twelve Scouts scurried to the yellow line and faced the lieutenant.

"Now, the first thing is we take off our hats because we don't want them blown into an engine or us to have to go chasing them down the ramp and run into a propeller." He took off his flight cap and secured it under his belt. The Scouts all did likewise.

Then, pointing out the walkway outlined in white, he said, "We want to always walk between the white lines. Make believe they're a sidewalk, and if you fall off, it's into a radioactive abyss."

"What's an abyss?" asked one of the Tenderfoot Scouts, squinting his eyes against the July sun.

"It's like a chasm," the lieutenant answered.

"Oh," said the Scout, no more understanding "chasm" than he had "abyss."

The lieutenant proceeded to give them the particulars of the C-124 Globemaster II, which of course they had all known since the day after the announcement two weeks ago that they would be visiting the flight line at Brookley Air Force Base. Tell a twelve- or thirteen-year-old boy he was going to see an airplane, and of course he'll find a way to know more about it than a pilot. Same thing with baseball statistics: all the boys were experts.

But then, there it was. The lieutenant had just said the C-124 was an original design when *everyone* knew it had been developed from the C-74 Globemaster I. Five hands shot up, each wanting to be the first to correct the lieutenant's error. The other seven boys kept their arms anchored in place, not wanting to draw attention to themselves. They were, after all, just Tenderfoot and Second Class Scouts. They knew not to outshine the First Class and Star Scouts that constituted the rest of the patrol.

At the end of the line, Second Class Scout "Three" Jackson had difficulty hearing the lieutenant over the ambient sounds of a flight line where the throbs of distant piston engines mixed with the high whine of jet engines and wafted in waves across the tarmac, with the sickly sweet smell of burning jet fuel somehow giving the sound an almost-liquid quality that permeated ears and noses. Unable to hear more than every third word, he let his eyes drift from the airplane—which he already had tons of pictures of—to the activity on the line: people under a C-124 working on the landing gear, others up on scaffolding working on engines, an F-89 Scorpion taxiing out for takeoff, and, landing on one of the runways, two new F-100 Super Sabres. He watched as the F-100s landed and taxied off the runway. They stopped, waiting for something, and then a blue pickup truck came tearing out from the ramp, turned in front of the two aircraft, and began to lead them as they made the transition from the active runway to the parking area. As the truck went past with the two screaming jets trailing behind it, Three saw a large sign in the rear of the truck that said "FOLLOW ME."

Later, inside the enormous belly of the C-124, where the flight line noises were more muffled, Three asked the lieutenant about the truck.

"Follow-me trucks are very important," the lieutenant explained. "When aircraft visit a base to which they are not assigned, it is almost impossible to give them directions to their parking spots, so we use a follow-me truck. The truck goes out to the runway and directs the aircraft along the best route to reach their parking spots in the shortest time and with the least amount of potential danger from running into other aircraft. The truck has a radio and is always talking to ground control. It's one of the most important functions we have on the flight line. You have to be a sergeant and pass a series of tests to be a follow-me driver."

Three was suitably impressed. He thought it would be good to be in charge, if only for the minutes it took to taxi a plane in from the runway.

The rest of the visit went as planned, with only one of the Scouts succumbing to the heat, noise, and smell of jet fuel, although when the first Scout started to vomit, the others nearly fell victim to losing their lunches as well.

Once away from the aircraft engines and exhaust, the inside of the bus seemed as quiet as the interval between the teacher announcing a pop quiz and the "awwwws" that follow. The seeming quiet, the effects of the July sun, and the early-evening hour caused a collective drowsiness, and as the bus reached home, the twelve somewhat-sunburned Scouts slept, contorted in their seats, dream-flying off into their own personal wild blue yonders. All, that is, save one, who was rushing around a dreamscape airdrome in his blue air force pickup with flashing lights and a large sign that said "FOLLOW ME."

⚜

*July 1959, Mound Victory, Alabama—north of Mobile*
His sunburn prickled when he splashed water on his face. He sure wished he had been able to wear his baseball cap, but even without it he had enjoyed climbing around the airplanes—especially the fighters. The one he found the most unusual, though, was the helicopter. It was brand new and had what they called counterrotating propellers. No, wait a second. They didn't call them propellers. They were—oh darn! What were they? Still, it was neat when the pilot came out and started it up and it took off. Even though he had never been in an airplane while it was flying, he thought that being close to the earth was the way to go. You could probably see better, and if something happened, you didn't have as far to fall.

"And speaking of earth, if I don't get out and weed that lettuce and cabbage, Daddy's going to take a belt to my behind," he thought.

As he hoed the rows of cabbage, he thought more about the helicopter. "Rotors!" he suddenly yelled. "That's what they called them. Rotors!"

He finished the last row of cabbage, raking into a pile what few weeds had grown, separating them out by hand, knocking the dirt off their roots, and throwing them into the compost pile behind the barn. He checked the fence for holes. It took just one rabbit to eat an entire row of cabbage or lettuce. He had just finished walking around the fence when his mother called him inside for breakfast.

He washed his hands on the porch. The screen door slammed behind him.

"Goddamn him! Goddamn the bank, and goddamn the county clerk!"

"Percy William Jackson! You sit down and watch your mouth! The children don't need to hear you cursing anyone!" His mother spoke as sternly to his father as she could. The more-than-a-foot difference in their heights made it so she had to lean her head back to look into his eyes. Hers flashed as his sought refuge from her look of castigation.

"Well, damn it, Linda Mae, this is their farm too. They have a right to know what the Gilberts are trying to do to us. Jacksons have been on this land since 1803, and I'll be damned if some carpetbagging Yankee is going to run me off like he did all my cousins."

"You know the Gilberts aren't carpetbaggers. Their people are from Tennessee."

"Just as bad. Tennessee didn't want to secede—and then when they did, they surrendered almost immediately. Hell! Andrew Johnson—and he was Lincoln's second vice president—was from Tennessee. In my mind, that makes anybody from Tennessee a Yankee and a carpetbagger."

"Well," his mother replied, "I don't want to lose the land either, but times are changing. Small farmers are losing out to big farmers, and big farmers are selling out to corporations. Won't be long before we're all working for some big conglomerate."

"Not in my lifetime! I'm going to find some way to beat these people even if I have to drive every last turnip, cabbage, tomato, and watermelon into Mobile and sell our produce on the street!"

He knew he couldn't do that though, because he had far more vegetables and fruit than he could ever get into the back of his two-and-a-half-ton truck. Plus, he didn't have enough labor to pack and load everything before it spoiled. Not being able to open his stand on Highway 43 this year was going to leave him with lots of spoilage and cut his income by at least a hundred dollars a day.

"Can't have a license for a stand if I don't own the road frontage! That's preposterous! I'm only a hill and a hollow off the highway, and the *county* owns that strip of right-of-way between the highway and the Gilberts' land where my stand should go. Damn Sonny for ever selling Liam Gilbert that corner anyway!"

His father went on throughout breakfast about how the Gilberts weren't going to let them open a fruit stand this year at the corner of Jackson Road and Highway 43. The Gilberts didn't grow vegetables, just corn—most of which went to feed the five hundred head of cattle they were running on the rest of the property that now surrounded the Jacksons' hundred acres. Pretty soon they'd want to change the name of the road that ran between Highway 43 and the Mobile River to Gilbert Road. Anyway, that's what his father said.

His father would have to try to sell more vegetables at the farmers' market in Mobile, but that meant getting up at three every morning, loading the truck, driving into Mobile, and renting a stall. A farmer barely made enough in a day to cover the cost of gas and the stall. It was tough for the truck farmers, and more and more of them were going out of business. Used to be some of them drove their trucks through the streets of Mobile, selling directly to the homeowners, but now with supermarkets being able to undersell even truck farmers, it was a dying business. Luckily, the Jackson farm wasn't mortgaged, but they did owe money on the three-year-old tractor and cultivator, without which they wouldn't be able to grow more than a few bushels of beans, peas, and corn.

"Won't even let us put up a sign telling people we have some of the best vegetables in the state! Damn them all!" His father rose, took his hat, and went back to the tractor, the screen door slamming behind him as an exclamation point.

After breakfast, Three went out to pick pole beans. While he was picking, he wondered how to get cars to come down

Jackson Road far enough to see some of the wonderful tomatoes and baskets of peas and beans displayed in front of the house. Whoever saw and tasted would buy. He had no doubts.

He mentioned it to his sisters, who at nine and ten picked the lower parts of the poles while he took the beans from the top.

"Well, I heard Daddy say they won't even let us put a sign out," said Lizzie, the older of the two. "If we could just put out a sign, people would come."

"But how would they know to come to our farm?" asked Shelby, the younger, who was trying to twist a difficult bean from the vine.

Three thought about signs. Too bad he didn't have a helicopter. Then he could hover overhead with a sign that said "Best Vegetables" with an arrow pointing down the road.

That afternoon he went to his Scout patrol meeting at the Boulangers, who lived two miles down Highway 43 toward Creola. Everyone talked about the trip to Brookley Field, but sometime during the meeting, talk got around to the Gilberts buying up property, and Three told the others what was happening at his house. He told them he didn't know how much longer his father could hold out.

"Well, you're welcome to put signs on Highway Forty-Three in front of my house, if you want," Mr. Boulanger told him. "At least that would get some northbound traffic looking for Jackson Road."

"Thank you. I'll tell my dad, but I know he'll think the southbound traffic headed into Mobile is the most important.

His theory is that people headed for home are most likely to stop and buy vegetables. Not the ones headed north toward Montgomery."

"Hey!" It was Fish Thompson, the Tenderfoot who had lost his lunch under the F-100 yesterday. "We live on Forty-Three just where State Road Eighty-Four comes in. I'm sure my dad won't mind if you put signs up there."

"Are you sure?" Three asked.

"Well, nobody likes the Gilberts buying up all the property around here," Mr. Boulanger said, "so why don't I call him and ask?"

A quick phone call, and Three was back on his bike, headed home to tell his dad.

The enthusiasm he hoped for didn't materialize. His father thought the Boulangers and Thompsons were too far away from Jackson Road for the signs to be effective. He really needed a sign at the corner with directions down the road. Without that, no one would want to turn off Highway 43. Still, he agreed Three and his sisters could take the signs they had used for years—ever since they first opened the vegetable stand on Highway 43—and try putting them up at the Boulangers' and the Thompsons'.

His dad was right. Nobody turned off.

Three went up to the corner to watch. He noticed cars slow down as if the drivers were looking for the old signs, but not seeing them, they sped up right away and drove past.

That night, Three dreamed about driving the follow-me truck again—only instead of leading jets, he was leading a long line of cars that weaved in and out of gigantic corn plants. He puzzled about it when he woke. Later, mucking out the milk cows' stall, he saw a thin plywood board that had "Follow the Arrows" printed on it.

Why not?

Taking the board, he painted it over with white paint and then carefully lettered it. He attached two canvas straps with staples so that the board would fit on his back like a cape, and got on his bike. He couldn't sit and pedal, because the board was too long, but if he stood and pedaled, the board rode nicely on his back.

At the corner, he waited for the first car to slow as if looking. Then he pedaled out, waving and pointing to the sign. He turned down Jackson Road and pedaled toward the vegetable stand. The first car ignored him, but the second turned down the road. Later, another joined the second in front of the new Jackson Road stand, and pretty soon each time Three pedaled up to the corner, he returned with another car. There was so much business his father had to stop his chores to help bag and sell the produce. His father answered questions about the tomatoes and the cantaloupe. Everyone loved his variety of purple tomatoes, and along with the tomatoes, the purple and green field peas were selling quickly. One man, driving a '58 Heavy Chevy Impala convertible, asked for a taste of a tomato. Three's dad washed one under the faucet and handed it to him. The man took a bite, juice cascading down his chin. His "Mmmmmm!" spoke volumes as he grabbed the lady with him by the shoulder and offered her a bite. He jammed the tomato into her face, juice spurting up under her eyes and around her cheeks.

"Are they all this good?" he asked Three's father.

"Well, it's late in the afternoon. The ones I pick in the morning will have a firmer set to the flesh and a chewiness to them. Not exactly crunchy, but they give you a bite as well as taste."

"How many are you picking?" the man asked.

"We could pick as many as five, maybe six bushels a day if you want them ripe and fresh."

"OK, now tell me about these purple field peas you have."

"Well, they're..."

By the time the man finished, he had contracted for daily supplies of tomatoes, field peas, pole beans, cantaloupes, yellow squash, mush melons, and sweet corn. He owned five restaurants in Mobile, in Prichard, and on the causeway—and he was always looking for the best produce. He wanted it daily, and he wanted it all summer. Did Mr. Jackson do any fall crops? How about winter squash? In one hour, the man had contracted for most of what the hundred-acre farm could produce.

If it wasn't a miracle, it came pretty close. They sold so much they had to take up the signs from the highway, and Three put away his bicycle-back sign, leaning it up against the stall fence. Printed on it was "Best Vegs—FOLLOW ME."

⚜

*November 1965, Mound Victory High School football field*
It couldn't happen. Nobody in the stands believed it would. Nobody on the Panthers' sideline believed it would. Nobody

listening on WABB radio believed it would. Nobody believed that little Mound Victory High School could beat the terror of Alabama football, the Mobile Panthers.

True, at 5–4–0, Mound Victory was having its best season in a decade, but the Mobile Panthers were 8–0–1, having been tied only by the other powerhouse in southern Alabama—the Fulton Yellowjackets—during the first week of the season. Since then, the Panthers had steamrolled over every opponent, and there was no reason Mound Victory would not be number nine. Mobile had more than two thousand students. Mound Victory had eight hundred—and that included freshmen.

With ten seconds left in the game, Mound Victory found itself on the Mobile nine-yard line with a third and goal, trailing the Panthers by four. They had been first and goal at the five, but a pass was broken up in the end zone, and then an attempted screen pass lost four yards when the quarterback was trapped trying to run out of a broken play. A field goal would do them no good, and besides, their starting center was on the bench—an ice bag on his neck from where a Panther linebacker elbow had dropped him.

In the huddle, the quarterback was at a loss as to what to call. He just stood there, his mouth open, sucking wind. The undersized fullback took charge. The senior, with blood running all over his jersey from his nose and a cut above his right eye, called, "Wing right, eight power right, on two." He repeated the call, and the players broke the huddle. As they were lining up, the coach saw the fullback grab the two-bar face mask of the left halfback and say something to him.

On the snap, the quarterback spun to his right and pitched the ball to the left halfback headed for the right end on a sweep. As the halfback caught the ball, a Panther linebacker came shooting through the line. Mound Victory's fullback gave him a glancing blow with his left forearm, just enough to knock him off stride. The linebacker recovered but only to pursue the halfback, who continued to sweep right. As the halfback reached the end of the line, he planted his right foot and pivoted down the field toward the end zone. As he did so, the fullback in front chucked the cornerback with his right shoulder, causing him to fall to the outside of the play. Next, the fullback took on Mobile's all-state safety. At six feet two inches, 215 pounds, the safety had four inches and thirty pounds on the fullback. The collision rocked the entire stadium. People in the parking lot could feel the shock wave. Radio listeners as far away as Baldwin County could hear the pads pop. The two players momentarily froze in time, helmet to helmet. Then the safety wavered, dropping to his knees as his left arm reached out feebly in an attempt to stop the running back.

On the snap, the play's impossibility was a foregone conclusion. At the five-yard line, success had become an improbable outcome, and at the two, it was still only a wished-for possibility. But in the end zone, it was a job well done. Mound Victory 12, Mobile 10.

Afterward the halfback was carried from the field on the shoulders of his teammates. Later he gave an interview to both the *Press-Register* stringer and the WABB announcer, and after that he had his picture taken with the homecoming queen and accepted all the laurels for leading his team to its first winning season in twelve years. He finally returned to the locker room. The last to shower and change, he would head off to whatever other victory ceremonies and tributes awaited the conquering hero.

But before he left, the coach found him. Slapping him on the shoulder, the coach told him how proud he was. Just before the halfback walked out the door, the coach asked, "On that last play, what did Three say to you when he grabbed your face mask?"

"Oh, nothing important, Coach. He just looked me in the eyes with that look he gets and said, 'Follow me.'"

⚜

*July 1968, Ton San Nhut Air Base, Republic of South Vietnam*
"Jackson, Percy W. the third!" The sergeant barked the name he read from the embarkation list.

"Here, Sergeant." Three responded as he grabbed his duffel bag and shuffled up the ramp of the CH-47 helicopter.

Throwing his duffel under the nylon sling seat, he collapsed with an effort into the seat, his fatigue pockets full of gear he couldn't get into his duffel bag. He felt awkward with so much extra stuffed into his pockets. This wasn't his first helicopter ride. He'd had plenty in training. But this helicopter was supposed to take him to where he'd start his year-long tour of duty with the army infantry in Vietnam.

"Percy? Did that man just call you Percy?" This from the man in front of him, whose name he thought he remembered as Hammerston or Hummerston or something like that.

"Yep, Percy is my given name, but most people just call me Three."

"Three? Where the hell you get a name like Three?"

"Easy. I'm the third, see? So instead of calling me Trey, like some people do, or Percy, they call me Three."

"Oh," said the soldier, not really seeing. "I'm Harry. Most folks just call me Harry."

"Hello, Harry. Where you headed?"

"Someplace called Bambi Touee or some such other. I suppose they'll tell me where it is when I get there. I learned in basic you're better off not asking questions in this army. Where you going?"

"Learned not to ask questions, huh?"

"Not to ask questions of sergeants and brass. You ain't either. Where you from?"

"Mound Victory, Alabama."

"You mean Mount Victory? We got one of those in Ohio."

"No, Mound Victory. Town's named after a skirmish in the Indian wars. A group of settlers were pursued by some renegade Creeks during the Red Stick uprising. The settlers found this mound and took a stand at the top of it. Turns out it was an Indian burial mound, and a lot of the Creeks wouldn't go up it, because it was holy ground and they were afraid. Seems some of the Creeks were half-breeds, including one who was a war chief. He and the medicine man had a big argument. He wanted the braves to charge the settlers, and the medicine man kept telling him if they did, they would die. Well, the war chief wanted to shame the rest of the group, so he and some other part-bloods charged up the mound. One of the settlers tried to shoot him but just got a fizz from his flintlock because of wet powder, so he took his tomahawk from his belt and threw it. It hit the war chief right in the middle of his chest, and he went head over heels down the mound, coming to rest at the feet of the medicine man. Well, the rest of the Creeks saw that as an omen and left quickly. Thus, it's Mound Victory, and the burial mound is in the center of town."

"Is that why you have an ax on your belt?"

"That's not an ax. It's a genuine fighting tomahawk."

"Oh," said Huddleston—or was it Hummerston?

"An Loc," said Three.

"What?"

"An Loc. That's where I'm going. It's over by the Cambodian border. I've got a pocket atlas of Vietnam, if you want to look up your village." Three tapped his shirt pocket but then remembered he had put the small atlas in one of the pouch pockets on his pants.

"No thanks. I'm just hoping I get to be the company clerk like they promised me when I signed up. Then I don't need to know anything except where the headquarters, latrine, and mess facilities are." Harry took his helmet off and inserted the earplugs they had given the soldiers as they signed in.

Just over a week ago, Three had landed in Vietnam on board an air force C-141. As he left the aircraft, walking off its rear ramp, the smells and sounds of Brookley Air Force Base came back to him. Burning jet fuel married with the sound of engines, propellers, and jets. The temperature was hot and the humidity high. Just like July in Mobile. He had already sweated through his fatigues, and he knew there would be salt stains when he finally took them off. As he walked down the ramp, he saw the follow-me truck speeding away from the front of the aircraft, headed out to pick up another transient transport delivering the buildup in army and marine corps troops to Vietnam. He wouldn't be an FNG long at this rate. "That's 'fucking new guy' to the uninitiated," he said to himself.

As the engines on the CH-47 started to whine, he could hear the rotors begin to turn—slowly at first, with an audible "whoosh" as each blade passed overhead. Then a constant whirr with a rocking gyration that bounced you up and down and in a circle at the same time. Then, suddenly, they were rolling, and the nose went down as the tail lifted, and they were flying. The ramp was open, so he could see the fields as they passed underneath the aircraft. Wind from the half-open crew door and windows in the front provided a cooling effect when combined with the sweaty wetness of his fatigues.

Their first stop was only minutes from Ton Sanut. They landed, and the sergeant directed four soldiers off the airplane. They took off once more and this time flew for almost an hour before they landed again. This time Huddleson or Hummerson—or whatever his name was—received directions to get off the chopper. Three knew they weren't anywhere near where the guy was going, so Harry would have to wait on a Huey to take him there.

They had to get off the aircraft at the next stop so it could be refueled. The base looked small, but it did have a perforated steel-plank runway from which some small observation aircraft, like O-1s and O-2s, were operating. As they took off, there was a really amazing sky to the west, where the sun was setting over the mountains. They flew into the deep orange pink of the sky while a light-purple darkness followed them. That had been the last stop before An Loc.

Three was in the last seat on the left side of the chopper. He sat half-turned in the seat so he could see clearly off the ramp as the bird passed over forest and field. The moon rose huge in the Eastern sky, almost full; its light hid the stars. Three could clearly see the land below. They were passing over rice paddies and what must have been ponds where people raised fish. There seemed to be scores of small round lights coming up from the ground as each pond and paddy reflected its own moon. He leaned farther out—his only connection to the aircraft being the seatbelt loosely secured across the tops of his thighs.

The first flash was partially shielded by the underside of the chopper. The second wasn't so much a flash as it was the helicopter rising quickly in the air, hanging there, and then quickly sagging down. He turned his head to the left and saw a fire up near the cockpit. It was like a flare had been set off inside the cabin. But this was no flare. It was an antiaircraft missile that had exploded near the door on the right-hand side of the aircraft. People in the front of the compartment slumped over, their arms and legs splayed in unnatural poses. There was no question the aircraft was in trouble. Its path was erratic, and its tail was swerving from side to side. Three held on to one of the bulkhead beams, but the gyrations were becoming so severe that the torque was cutting his hand on the aluminum. The fire was working its way backward; people were screaming. For some reason he loosened his belt and stepped off the back of the ramp. He wouldn't burn; he just wouldn't.

He fell.

It wasn't as far as he thought. He hit the water feetfirst, feeling like his tibias were being driven up through his chest. The wind was knocked completely out of him. He didn't exactly lose consciousness, but he did lose his sense of up and down, left and right. He struggled to right himself only to find he was wrapped in vines or lines. He did not sink any farther, and after what seemed hours, he realized he was lying in water completely covered in large lily pads. It was the stems of the pads in which he had become tangled. It wasn't a rice paddy, so it must have been one of the ponds where the locals raised fish. Pulling at the stems, he noticed his feet could touch the bottom; the water reached only just over his shoulders. But he did have to extract his feet from the mud, of which there was at least two feet. Afterward, he would credit the lily pads and mud for breaking his fall as much as, or more than, the water.

He had seen the helicopter continuing onward, its burning fuselage lighting the sky. It was only afterward, though, that the vision actually registered in his brain. For the time being, he simply stood neck-deep in lily pads, mud, and water, trying to recover his breath and to keep from falling facedown.

After what must have been hours, he tried to walk. His right leg, then his left leg. His right arm, then his left. He hurt, but once he could breathe again, the pain was not excruciating. It wasn't any worse than the second day of blocking and tackling during two-a-day football practices in high school. He made his way to the edge of the pond. It was hardly darker than twilight, with the moon now past its zenith and well on its way to setting. With the moon smaller, he could see thousands of stars as well.

Not really thinking, upon reaching drier land—which was a little inaccurate because he was in what appeared to be terraced rice paddies—he instinctively followed the path he had seen the helicopter taking. It hadn't appeared to deviate from its course, so if he continued in a straight line, he should, sooner or later, find where it had landed (he hoped) or crashed (he feared).

Because he was skirting each rice paddy, the trek took longer than it would have had he been able to walk in a straight line, but he had the adrenaline of the fall and safe landing pumping through his arteries and veins, so while he ached, he did not feel tired. He navigated by selecting a landmark in front of him and then walking to it. Once there, he would pick another as his horizon advanced.

At daybreak, he had to take greater care, for now he could see an occasional person, and his route became more circuitous as he had to give each person a wide berth. He had lost his rifle, but he still had his fighting knife and his tomahawk securely fastened to his web belt. However, never having killed anyone, he wasn't convinced he could do it, especially with a knife or tomahawk. Still, he was experienced in stalking from his hunting and Boy Scout days. He hoped he would not be tested on whether he could use his weapons on a human.

His watch still worked, and he had three or four candy bars in his fatigue pockets, as well as matches and tinder in a waterproof container, a flashlight, the pocket atlas, a sewing kit, and three fruit-and-nut bars from a C ration. The fruit-and-nut bars were hard as rock, and most people didn't like them. But he did. He found chewing on them with a little water was a great way to stave off real hunger. Besides, he didn't like the other choices the C or K rations provided. The pork was vile, as were most of the other meat choices. He had a baby bottle full of water in the thigh pocket of his fatigues. Just something suggested to him by a friend's friend who had already served his tour somewhere down in the Delta. It was only ten ounces, but that was better than nothing. He had two bottles of iodine tablets as well, so he could purify water as needed. While he was fishing in his pockets for the small iodine bottles, he pulled out the pen flare gun he had been issued. It was the size of a ballpoint pen and shot .38-caliber flares. Five flares were attached to the lanyard. He could, if necessary, shoot a flare horizontally as a weapon—although it was very difficult to aim.

By his watch, he stopped at eight o'clock and, crawling inside a bush that had no thorns, watched for half an hour while he gnawed on one of the fruit bars. He sipped the water even though he knew he should go ahead and drink it down, replacing the water and placing one or two of the iodine tablets in it. Still, he couldn't bring himself to drink the rice paddy water. It looked even worse than the black water of the bayous off the Mobile River.

At nine o'clock he knew he was getting close to the CH-47. The number of people he could see had increased, and there was a road running down the mountain to a hollow and then out onto what appeared to be some sort of river plain. Concealing himself, he pulled out his pocket atlas, and after fifteen minutes of gently separating the still-wet pages, he believed he had identified his location. If he was correct, An Loc was another forty miles to the west. There must be aircraft out looking for the now-much-overdue CH-47, but scanning the sky, he saw none.

Working the ridgelines and keeping himself just below the summit so as not to appear as a silhouette against the sky, he moved above the road until he could see the CH-47 down in the middle of the road. Its middle third appeared to have burned to the ground, and the two main rotors leaned in toward the middle. The cockpit and tail appeared intact, but there was a large gathering around what remained of the helicopter, and Three could see what appeared to be soldiers. Then he remembered the small opera-sized, eight-powered field glasses he had received as a high school graduation present. He had stuffed them in his breast pocket. He took them out, made sure they weren't broken, and zoomed in on the scene below him.

Sure enough, there were what appeared to be Vietcong in their black pajamas and coolie hats, each armed with an AK-47, all around the aircraft. Momentarily, his still-somewhat-addled brain noted the irony of an AK-47 being used to guard a CH-47—and that 1947 was the year of his birth.

Looking beyond the aircraft to the far side of the valley, he saw a group of prisoners linked one to another by ropes around their necks and with burlap-like bags over their heads. Their hands were bound, and they were sitting on the edge of the road. They were all barefoot. From the uniforms, he could tell they were the crew and some of the passengers he had departed with from Ton Sanut.

He concealed himself again and waited. He ate a candy bar and sipped the water. He had five ounces left. He watched. He concentrated at first on each of the prisoners. One or two seemed uninjured, but all the others seemed to have an issue with an arm or a leg. It seemed strange that the Vietcong hadn't moved them from the crash site yet. Someone with a camera was moving along the line, pulling the bag off each prisoner's head and taking his picture. Then the photographer would put the bag back on and moved to the next. There were fourteen prisoners. Three tried to remember how many people had been on the CH-47 before the antiaircraft fire. Certainly more than fourteen.

Three had been careful to reconnoiter the rest of the slope he was on and the slope across from him. He noted there were several two-man teams deployed around the valley with what appeared to be shoulder-fired antiaircraft missiles. That wasn't good. There was little chance a rescue team could get into the valley if it was defended with shoulder-fired missiles. That was why they hadn't moved yet. They were waiting to see if more aircraft would come.

At five o'clock—by Three's watch—a group of seven Vietcong started shouting and gesticulating at the prisoners to get up. They prodded them with the barrels of the rifles, and one went so far as to strike one of the prisoners with the butt of his AK. Interestingly, he was immediately chastised by his superior. Apparently they wanted these prisoners in good shape for interrogation. At least for now, the prisoners seemed safe.

They made each prisoner put his hand on the shoulder of the person in front of him and then began to march them off down the road, toward where the hollow opened out into the river plain. It wasn't difficult for Three to stay a little ahead of them, because the prisoners moved slowly.

Still there were no aircraft.

By eight o'clock the prisoners and their guards had almost reached the river plain where the forest ended and the entire flat area was given over to rice paddies. It looked as if they would stop for a while, since two or three individuals built small, smokeless fires under the edge of the triple-canopy forest.

Three had no idea how he should proceed. Should he attempt to bypass the group and make his way to An Loc? By the time he made it, the group would have gone in some other direction, and his information would be of little use. If he shadowed the group until they reached their destination, he risked being captured or led days away from US or other friendly forces that might effect a rescue.

He settled down inside a bush, gnawed on a fruit bar, and watched. The group put pickets out. He could see where each of the guards was positioned to protect the perimeter of the group.

As night settled, the moon—only slightly less bright than it had been the night before—allowed him to continue to see the two closest pickets. He edged down the slope slowly until he could smell the small fires as the aroma of burning wood made its way sideways under the tree canopy. The prisoners were at the east end of the makeshift camp—meaning they would have to go through the camp to exit in the direction of An Loc. If he could free the prisoners, he would have to keep them on flat terrain, if possible, since several appeared gimpy and going up the slope would be difficult for them.

How could he draw most of the soldiers out of the camp long enough for him to get the prisoners away?

Then he heard it. Somewhere from the west, an aircraft was approaching. He moved quickly back up the slope, searching the sky to the west. He could see it silhouetted against the sky. Pilots didn't like nights like this, because bright moonlight made them easy to spot. Bright, cloudless nights produced what the pilots called "gunners' moons." Three didn't know what kind of aircraft it was. If it was just a cargo aircraft, it might not be paying attention to the ground. If, on the other hand, it was an FAC—forward air controller—this might be an opportunity.

He took the pen gun from his pocket and screwed in a flare. He pulled the pin back into the locked position and held the pen straight up over his head. The last thing he wanted to do was point it at the aircraft, because the small flare could be interpreted as a tracer round being fired at the aircraft—and the last thing he needed was a bunch of fast-moving jets attacking his position with bombs and rockets.

He released the pin, and the flare climbed quickly into the sky, its red tail pointed down to his position. He saw the aircraft begin a turn, but at the same time, the ground around him erupted in a series of thuds as someone fired at him from below. He heard voices shouting. He moved quickly, keeping the encampment below him and on the other side of the road. Now he wanted the ridgeline, so he went up. The other side of the ridge was what he needed.

Looking over his shoulder, he could see the muzzle flashes of the AKs from below, and he could hear the splats and thuds as the rounds tore into the ground where he had been hiding. Nearing the ridge, he dropped to his stomach and started to low-crawl across the top, reducing his silhouette to keep from being spotted. Once on the other side, he wiggled down just far enough so he could stand up and run. The aircraft had dropped lower. He could tell it was a C-123, probably a night FAC looking for trucks on the road. He stopped long enough to launch another flare and then kept running toward where the ridge began to dip down to the plain.

Without consciously thinking, he was attempting to place himself ahead of the group of prisoners. He knew that if the

VC thought their position was compromised, they would move the prisoners quickly. That they had been moving westward since they started meant they would probably keep doing so—at least until the road hit the plain. He had to make it to the road and try to do something until help arrived.

The C-123 had started circling. He had to find an open spot where he could shoot a flare so the pilots could see him. If they would just hang around long enough for him to reach the road at the bottom. He was running as fast as he could, stumbling over rocks and roots, his fatigues catching on branches. He fell and got up. He ran; he fell and tumbled; he got up; he ran.

Finally, the ground began to level out, and the trees thinned. He was on the edge of a large rice paddy farm. The C-123 was making large oval orbits.

He drew the pen from his pocket and sent up a third flare. This time he stayed in position. The C-123 moved in, dropping lower. Three remembered the flashlight in his pocket. He took it out and, making sure he had the red lens on, began to flash *dot-dot-dot, dash-dash-dash, dot-dot-dot*. The C-123 was headed directly for him. He could see a red light in the cockpit window. It flashed. As the C-123 passed overhead, it wiggled its wings and began to climb. It moved off to the west but kept orbiting.

If Three did nothing more he would be safe. All he had to do was hide till morning, and they would send in a rescue force. But there was no way he could accept being safe as long as the Vietcong held the fourteen others.

The group would have to come out of the valley to the south of his location. He needed something to slow them down and create confusion. He needed to separate the prisoners from their guards somehow.

He knew they wouldn't travel on the road but off to one side. Probably on the same side they had been walking earlier. At some point, he knew, they would meet up with transport. Probably somewhere near the Cambodian border.

He had thought about this constantly before he enlisted, during basic and advanced infantry training. Would he be able to kill? After all, he didn't even know these people. Why would he want to kill them? Then he said to himself, "Well, they don't know me either, and any of those rounds earlier could have killed me." It wasn't a good resolution, but it was a good-enough rationalization. He didn't know any of the prisoners either, but for some reason he was willing to die to free them. Something he could ruminate about in old age. Assuming, of course, he reached old age.

How would they come? As a group? Or would they put flankers out? If they deployed flankers, he could take out the flanker on the north side of the road and then use the flanker's AK. No, that wouldn't work. One AK against six wasn't good odds. Besides, these guys knew the terrain, and they were experienced.

He could take out one flanker—he knew he could—but then what to do? He needed to draw the majority of the team away from the prisoners. Then it struck him that the old cowboy trick might work. He worked his way back up the north side of the road, and out of sight of the path, he took the back side of his tomahawk and dug a twelve-inch hole into which he put twigs and small branches. He then made his way back to the path. For some reason, he picked up a handful of dirt and rubbed it over his face and the backs of his hands.

The flanker was looking, but he was looking down at the road, not up the slope. He passed Three, who quickly ran up behind him and struck him between the shoulder and neck with the broadside of his tomahawk. The flanker fell like a sack of rice falling off a cart. Three didn't know why he had turned the tomahawk at the last second. It had started out with its keenly honed killing blade aimed for the man's neck.

Regardless, the flanker was on the ground and would be for some time. Three took the man's AK and searched his body for the extra magazine. He pulled the flanker off the trail and up the slope, hiding him under a large plant with elephant ear–like leaves. He returned to the hole he had dug, shucked all but a few rounds of the ammo out of the two magazines he had found, and deposited them onto the ground beside the hole. He slung the AK over his shoulder. He dropped two matches onto the brush in the hole. It caught quickly. He used his boot to push the fifty or so rounds of ammo into the hole with the fire and then quickly made his way back toward where the trail joined the road as it exited the valley.

He looked for the next flanker up the slope on the south side and saw movement in the brush. Taking his greatest chance so far, he crossed the road in a low crawl and then headed up the slope. The flanker was moving slowly, trying not to get too far ahead of the main group. Three moved upslope from him just as the ammo in the hole started to cook off. It sounded like a real firefight. The flanker spun to look. Three came down the slope and again laid a Vietcong out with the broadside of his tomahawk. He took this man's AK too, sticking the extra ammo clip inside his web belt. He put the tomahawk back under his belt and started upslope again. When he got far enough up, he moved toward the group. He found the prisoners, bags over their heads, huddled together. One Vietcong was pointing his rifle at them and yelling in Vietnamese. The other four Vietcong had run toward the sounds of shooting. The Vietcong with the prisoners kept looking over his shoulder in their direction. He was obviously nervous. He was also very young. Three could have shot him, but instead he used the group of prisoners to shield his approach, and when the young VC turned to look again, Three coldcocked him with the butt of the second AK.

He quickly pulled the bags off the heads of the prisoners with one hand as he used his fighting knife to cut the ropes on the hands of the first in line. Everyone began to speak, but Three, using his best fullback voice, said firmly, "QUIET," then more quietly, "Cut yourselves free. Someone take this VC's rifle and ammo. Follow me."

They moved out quickly in the direction of the plain. They had difficulty, but Three kept them moving. He figured daylight was at least two hours off. Reaching the end of the valley, he led them across the road and toward the north, where they gathered in a small opening. The C-123 continued its high orbit. Three took out his pen gun and shot his fourth flare. The

C-123 began to descend, and as it approached, Three used his flashlight to signal *dot-dash-dash-dash-dash*, then *dot-dot-dot-dot-dot*. Morse code for fifteen. As the aircraft flew over, the survivors who could waved their arms. Once again, the C-123 wiggled its wings as it began to climb.

Three moved the group further westward. Skirting the rice paddies was both difficult and time consuming. In less than thirty minutes, he could see figures coming out of the tree lines and into the paddies. By the way the figures moved, he could tell they were Vietcong and not early-morning workers.

The C-123 was no longer there. "Probably fuel," Three said to himself.

His group had three AKs now but only four and a half clips of ammo. Not enough for a firefight, but maybe enough to slow the pursuers down a little. Although there were a captain, a lieutenant, and two warrant officers in the group, they continued to follow Three as if he had been appointed to command. They had minor burns and were still a little disoriented, but they certainly understood what was happening.

Three didn't know where the Vietcong had found so many others in such a short time, but now there were definitely two dozen or so. He continued to move his group to the west, but they were gradually being overtaken. Then he heard the first round overhead as their pursuers began to fire at them across the paddies.

The sky had begun to lighten in the east. The stars had all but disappeared, and the moon had set. "How long?" he wondered. "If we go to ground here, they'll flank and then encircle us." Still, he could not risk exposing his slow-moving group to any type of concentrated fire, and in the paddies, at least he could see on all four sides. He ordered everyone into the water.

They all dropped into a paddy. Three, remembering his familiarization training with the AK, checked to see the magazine was seated securely, pushed the safety selector switch to semi, and pulled the charging lever. He figured the closest Vietcong was about three hundred meters away, so he sighted slightly above him. He pulled the trigger. The round must have hit somewhere close, because the Vietcong dropped into a rice paddy. Three then pointed his AK at others and loosed off five rounds in quick succession. He told the two other survivors with rifles not to fire. They would hold those in reserve.

Now the waiting game began, with occasional rounds exchanged as the Vietcong moved to flank Three's group. He could see a coolie hat to his right and then one to his left about four hundred yards off. He shot at the one on the right.

Then an L-19/O-1 Bird Dog observation aircraft appeared at about five thousand feet. Three rolled over on his back and, fixing his last flare, fired it straight up. All the Vietcong began firing at the aircraft, standing to do so. As they did, Three fired a burst at the two closest. They dove back into their paddies. In the distance he could see many more coolie hats coming from the woods and into the paddies, and rounds began to kick up water and earth all around the paddy where Three's group was hiding.

He could hear them coming several miles off, like distant thunder. As the sound got louder, the O-1 made a slight diving motion and fired off some marking rockets toward the Vietcong positions. And then the thunder arrived: F-100 Super Sabres, not unlike those Three had seen at Brookley AFB. Only these were painted in camouflage green, and as they flew overhead, they released several streamlined devices that looked a great deal like bombs. The tree line and the first row of paddies erupted in bright orange, which then turned into black smoke with orange flames shooting up through it. The inferno sucked the air from all around—even from as far away as Three's paddy. Napalm.

After the F-100s, a flight of A-1s roared in, their twenty-millimeter wing guns flashing. Their rounds impacted near Three's group. There were Vietcong on three sides of them—some as close as a hundred yards. The A-1s pulled up and around, now crossing the valley on the perpendicular. This time they fired 2.75-inch rockets with antipersonnel warheads. All of the coolie hats to the right and left of Three dove for the cover of the nearest rice paddy. Many of them did not reappear.

As he had heard the F-100s, Three could now hear the Hueys. The slap of their rotor blades was all the louder against the wet morning air. They appeared out of the west, flying low, and three of them dropped into the paddies on either side of Three's group.

The sound of AK rounds striking the helicopters was like bees flying into closed windows. Three was helping those with arm injuries get into the choppers when the AK round struck him in the lower-right part of his back. It passed through his lung, breaking a rib, and exited just to the right of his navel.

He crawled onto the floor of the Huey and lay there. "So close," he whispered.

The MASH (mobile army surgical hospital) unit at An Loc. A C-7 flight to Saigon. Then a C-141 medical evacuation aircraft to the Philippines, and finally another C-141 to Brook Army Medical Hospital in San Antonio, Texas. Three had surgery to repair the torn tissue and collapsed lung. The army had no further use for his service, and he was prepped to be medically discharged. Perhaps his was the shortest tour ever in Vietnam. But the army wasn't quite finished with him. At Fort Benning, Georgia, they held a ceremony. There were some generals, Three's congressman from Alabama, his family, one or two friends from Mound Victory, and a couple of the other passengers who had been on the CH-47. They presented Three with a Purple Heart and the Distinguished Service Cross for heroism. They took pictures on the stage in the auditorium. Three stood there with his parents under a large scroll that read, "I am the Infantry. Follow Me."

⚜

*July 2013, Church of the Holy Comforter, Mound Victory, Alabama*

The small Episcopal church had seats for only a hundred people; thus it was that the windows were opened so those who ringed the church outside could hear and participate. They fanned themselves with paper fans, for it was a typical Alabama July day. Hot and humid. Men shucked their coats, standing in shirt sleeves. As many women as possible had been accommodated in the pews, but many more stood in the side aisles and on the steps as well. No one had prepared to have a thousand people in a hundred-person church, but there they were. They came not because he had gained fame; he hadn't. Nor did they come because he was rich. He wasn't. They came because they were his friends, and they came to celebrate a life.

A choir up from Mobile sang "Mansions of the Lord." One bishop read the service, and another prayed for his soul—but made the point that perhaps those gathered should not be praying for the soul of the departed but should be entreating the departed to pray for their souls.

Fish Thompson described how Three had used his GI bill to go to Auburn and study agriculture. How he had married a lovely young coed and had come home to a hundred acres in Mound Victory. A succession of other friends and former clients—who had become friends—told how he had become the county agricultural agent and led the grange to design and develop its own soybean processing plant, initially producing a spray used to keep down road dust on unimproved secondary roads, then producing flash-frozen soybeans, and finally manufacturing woven products from soy plant fibers. They told how the county had prospered and how Three had been drafted to run for representative and then state senator.

A state senator delivered a eulogy that sounded more like an election speech—telling how in Montgomery Three had been one of the leaders in the legislative effort to bring foreign investors into Mobile and Huntsville and to export the county's soy-based technology to many other counties in the state. How he had insisted that parts of the Gulf Coast be kept from developers so that beaches were still accessible to those tourists who could not afford the pricey resorts and condo complexes. When the senator finished, everyone there was ready to vote Three back into office.

Another state senator described how Three had refused drafts for higher office because he would have had to leave Rotary, the Kiwanis, Little League, and his parish church.

A zone officer from Rotary recounted how Three had become a Rotary Club president, assistant district governor, and district governor but had resisted drafts for higher Rotary office because he felt it more important to do good locally than internationally, reasoning that if you set examples locally, others would take that example to the international arena.

And every speaker echoed how Three always had time for anyone with a problem and a dollar for anyone down on his or her luck. How his children were as successful as they were nice.

And then Three's wife told them about how at age sixty Three found out he had leukemia. Not ordinary leukemia but a rare type that generally struck only children. How he went to Saint Jude's in Memphis and offered to be a guinea pig for treatment and drugs since he was bigger and stronger than the children. And how he fought the disease for five years before it wore him down.

She did not cry, even though many in the congregation made no attempt to hold back their tears. Rather, she stood tall and spoke with purpose in her voice. She was determined that people see in her husband what she had seen and loved all these years.

As they processed from the church to the graveyard, the choir sang,

> Once to every man and nation
> Comes the moment to decide,
> In the strife of truth with falsehood
> For the good or evil side.

The coffin was placed on the frame; the flag was removed, folded, and presented to his wife. The honor guard fired a volley, and as the casket was lowered, the headstone became visible to those gathered round. It read:

> Percy William Jackson III
> 1947–2013
> Follow Me

# A Real First Captain and More

⚜

I LOOKED AT MY NEW watch. It was ten past four. The light had already gone from what little sky could be seen from the manmade canyons of New York City. The portico of the Waldorf Astoria was brightly lit. My feet were cold. The pavement was cold, and the cold seeped through the soles of my shoes. My nose was cold and runny. My fingers were stiff but still a little warm in the gloves Uncle Charlie had given me, since I was spending so much time wiping my nose that my fingers didn't have a chance to get too cold. Still, December 30, 1958, was finishing up as one of the coldest days of my eleven years.

I had stood at the Waldorf most of the day, and the day before as well, but had not seen General MacArthur. The day before, when I first came, I tried to bribe Michael, the doorman, with one of the remaining pimento cheese sandwiches Aunt Belle had prepared for our trip. The sandwich was in my pocket. It was only a little stale. The doorman laughed and, after a bit, agreed that if the general was going out, he would tell me when they called down for his car. Unfortunately, when I arrived just before noon the next day, the doorman told me the general had already gone out not a half hour before. Well, at least I knew the general was out. He had to return. So I was standing where the doorman assured me I would be out of trouble's way. I continued to wait.

I occasionally talked to some of the bellmen as they carried luggage in and out of the hotel. There was Tony from Jersey and Arnold from "Da Bronx." Arnold really talked like one of the Bowery Boys. Yet in my young, inexperienced mind, the Bronx was a bit removed from the Bowery. I planned to test this theory the next morning. I would take the subway to the Bowery, and I would determine if the Bowery boys might really have been from the Bronx or if they talked funny in the Bowery as well. Arnold was happy being a bellman, but Tony wanted to be called Anthony because he thought he could move up faster if his name was a little more formal. He was trying to talk the bell captain into giving him a new name tag. Only when Tony and Arnold said "Anthony," it seemed to come out more like "Antny." I didn't think that was much of a formal name, but then, I was not from New York.

The bell crew didn't mind me, because I explained that while I had come to New York City with my father on business, my real reason was to meet Douglas MacArthur, general of the army. I explained how General MacArthur was one of the greatest generals in the history of the country. They pretty much agreed with me, and besides, they had come to think of me as a minor celebrity in my own right. I had mentioned that on Sunday, after arriving on Saturday, my father and I had gone to see the New York Giants play the Baltimore Colts in the World Championship football game. It had been a surprise for both of us. When we arrived at the hotel, the tickets had been waiting. They were a gift from the potential business client my father would be meeting.

So on Sunday, my father and I stood in Yankee Stadium. Nobody sat, not from the time everyone rose for the national anthem. The game was too exciting. And besides, being short, I had to stand just to see. It was the first championship ever to go to overtime.

We rooted for the Giants, partly because we thought it proper to root for the home team since we were, after all, in New York and I had never even been to Baltimore. My father had, but he said it didn't really count because it was a business trip. But mostly we rooted for the Giants because they had Charlie Conerly at quarterback. He was from Mississippi, and he served valiantly as a marine in the war before returning to Ole Miss. The Colts quarterback Johnny Unitas was from Pittsburgh, Pennsylvania. We didn't begrudge Mr. Unitas his chance at glory, and since there were no professional football teams in the South, we recognized that Baltimore (and the Washington Redskins) came the closest to being home teams for whom we southern boys and dads might cheer. Still, my father and I thought we should cheer for someone who was from somewhere a little closer to home than Baltimore or Pittsburgh.

By the time Baltimore's Alan Ameche went over right tackle for the game-winning touchdown, both my father and I were too cold to care. Later, our hotel suite seemed like an oven, and we felt like frozen dinners. After thawing out, we were too tired for anything but sandwiches from Aunt Belle's basket—and bed.

Still, the bell crew accorded me minor hero status, for tickets to the "Greatest Game Ever Played," as the newspapers were calling it, had been impossible to come by. Many guests at the Waldorf had been most disappointed when the concierge could not supply them. "Isn't this the Waldorf? I stayed here specifically because I was told the Waldorf could get you tickets for anything." One of the guests had made this pronouncement somewhat piercingly on Saturday. Or so Tony told me.

I checked my watch again. It was a Waltham wristwatch my grandfather had given me two years before. It kept good time if I remembered to wind it. I didn't really have to look at the watch, though, because there was a ship's clock just behind the bell captain's desk, and it, too, read fifteen minutes after four. My father and I had agreed to meet in front of the Waldorf at four thirty. There were only fifteen minutes left. Getting warm wouldn't be much of a consolation prize if I didn't get to meet General McArthur, I thought, but it would be better than not seeing the general and staying cold. I simply could not imagine how people in the North lived there in the winter.

My camera was heavy around my neck. I had practiced holding it up, snapping a photo, and winding the winding knob without taking my eye from the viewfinder. I had several pictures of the doorman and the bell captain, as well as Tony and Arnold. I hoped the bright lights of the Waldorf entrance would make up for my not having a flash. The camera didn't come with one.

At 4:25, a large black Cadillac drew to the curb. The doorman gave me the high sign as he moved to open the rear passenger-side door. I looked for the general, but there was only an old man in a dark wool coat in the car. He exited the car slowly, a cane in his right hand. As he turned slightly to avoid the door edge, he came into profile, and his aquiline nose was unmistakable. He was, Douglas MacArthur, general of the army. The general straightened; he placed one of those funny hats—either a humbug or a hamburger, I believed—on his head. He spoke to the doorman. "Well, Mick, how's the family?"

"Just fine, General," Mick said. "Thank you for asking. Uh, General, you have an admirer who has waited most of yesterday and today to get a picture." He nodded in my direction. Good ole Mick!

"This is it!" I thought. The general looked at me. I was petrified. I neither snapped to attention nor extended my hand. He asked, "And what is your name, young man?"

Name! Name? That was not part of my rehearsed role. I had not anticipated the general would ask my name.

He switched his cane to his left hand and proffered his right. It was large. Much larger than mine. They say training will save you when an emergency occurs. Indeed, it did. My training as a young southern gentleman kicked in, and I took his hand in mine. I grasped it firmly but not too firmly. I pumped it once and withdrew my hand.

I managed to say, "Pleased to meet you, sir." And then that training, with its ten years of repetition, kicked in again. "My name is Jack...Jack Jourdain. I'm from Mobile, Alabama."

"And I am pleased to meet you, Jack. Does that camera work?"

Camera? What camera? My mind sought answers. Oh, yes, the one hanging from my neck.

"Yes, sir, it works."

"Well then, perhaps Mick can take a picture of us. Would you like that?"

We southern boys might stagger from the first blow, physical or metaphysical, but our southern mothers didn't raise wimps. I had recovered.

"Absolutely, sir," I replied. I was my father's son and my grandfather's grandson.

I handed Mick the camera and said, "General, my great-grandfather had the honor to be in Chattanooga when your father won the Medal of Honor."

"Did he now? What was his regiment?"

"The Forty-First Alabama, sir. He was a lieutenant. He was eighteen years old."

"And my father was nineteen. That seems fitting. And you, young Jack, will you be a soldier?"

"It is my intention, sir, to go to West Point. I shall try to become first captain, as you were." We were standing next to one another; the general had his right hand on my left shoulder.

In his left hand he held his cane loosely. He did not use it to steady himself.

A flash went off. My camera didn't have a flash. Little balls of light traveled about my eyes. The balls of light moved to the center of wherever I tried to look. The hand was off my shoulder, and I felt my right hand being shaken again. There was another flash.

"Well, Jack, I wish you the greatest of luck in your endeavors."

"Thank you, sir." I snapped to attention and saluted.

He raised his cane, now back in his right hand, to the brim of his humbug—or was it hamburger?—hat. Mick opened one of the side doors of the hotel, and the general strode through.

I stood, hand still in salute, until he disappeared. "Ready, two." I thought of the military command and dropped my hand to my side.

A man in a suit with a press camera handed me a slip of paper. "The photographs will be ready in two hours. You can pick them up at the concierge desk," he said. I looked at Mick. He was smiling as if he had just won the Derby lottery.

"I thought the hotel might like to have a picture of the general's fan club," he said. "After all, this is the Waldorf." His uniform buttons shone brightly in the lights of the portico. He rushed to help a lady exit the hotel. She needed a cab, so he went to the curb and blew his whistle. From down the street a yellow cab appeared. He opened the door for the lady. She handed him a dollar bill. He touched the brim of his cap and returned. He was still smiling.

The photographs had caused a small crowd to form on either side of the portico. I heard people speaking.

"Who is he?"

"I don't know. Who do you think he is?"

"Who was that who went through the door?"

From the edge of this small crowd, my father stepped into the lights of the portico.

"So you did get to meet the general."

There were too few words available to an eleven-year-old to explain my feeling. My father shook Mick's hand and introduced himself. Mick handed him my camera. Tony walked by with some luggage on a cart and said hello. I felt my father's hand on my shoulder guiding me away from the bright lights.

"The pictures!" I blurted out.

"Won't be ready until later. They have your name. I gave it to Mick. They'll hold them for us. Let's eat early. There's a nice small restaurant a few blocks over."

Seated at the table, I still hadn't said more than "Hot chocolate, please" and "I prefer blue cheese dressing, if you have it."

My father had been quiet as well. He sipped the Manhattan he ordered.

"Well, Jack," he said. He didn't call me "boy" or "son" as he normally did. "Well, Jack, you did it. But then, I'm not really surprised. Your life has always had those special, brief, charm-like episodes. And I have no reason to believe it will not continue to be so."

The hot chocolate had warmed me to the point I began to revive. I nudged myself away from imagining the possibilities of the future and back into the real world.

"Dad, he wished me luck in my endeavors. General MacArthur wished me not just luck but the greatest of luck. He said, 'Jack, I wish you the greatest of luck in your endeavors.' The greatest of luck!"

My father looked over his glass at me. Our eyes locked, his deep black eyes and my still-forming green ones.

"Yes, he did, Jack. He wished you luck. And you know the definition of luck, don't you? We've talked about it scores of times."

"Yes, sir. Luck is the intersection of preparation and opportunity."

"Yes, it is, Jack. Remember that. And as the general said, the greatest of luck in your endeavors."

---

"A Real First Captain and More" originally appeared as chapter 4 in the author's first novel, *The Train*.

# BETWEEN HEAVEN AND HELL

⚜

HE WOULD FREEZE IF HE could not find refuge. Hadn't they taught him how to make a snow cave in survival training? But if he stopped, he would freeze. If only he could see where he was going. He must be in an ice fog. He couldn't see ahead, but it was extremely bright, as if the sun was shining through the fog. He thought he could make it out. The sun was almost directly overhead, but that couldn't be. For it to be this cold, he would have to be too far north for the sun to be in that position. How did he get here? He was in Texas, wasn't he? Maybe he was in the panhandle. "It gets cold in the panhandle," he thought. He involuntarily shivered again. "Too cold."

He was very tired. He needed to sleep. Just a minute or two. If he could just stop. But somehow he knew he mustn't. He must go on, but it was so cold. He must stay upright. He kept going. Was that a sound?

It sounded like a muffled pounding. He could feel the vibrations. In the distance was the sound of mumbled murmurings. Perhaps voices, but perhaps an ocean. There were no oceans in Texas. Maybe he was near the Gulf—but he could not be so cold at the Gulf. He searched his memory for somewhere so cold and barren but could think only of Dante, and the thought frightened him. Was his life so irredeemable that God would condemn him to the innermost circle of hell?

He couldn't remember how he had gotten from his airplane to this place. He must have ejected, but he didn't remember it. In fact, he couldn't actually remember being in the plane. His feeling was more akin to assuming he had been. If only the fog would lift and he could see. The light was so bright it hurt his eyes. If it was the sun, he instinctively knew he must watch closely. They always came at you out of the sun. He himself always attacked out of the sun. But he couldn't seem to keep his eyes open. Yet he knew he must keep going. He did not feel out of breath, his muscles did not hurt, there was no pain—but he was so very sleepy, so very tired, and so very, very cold.

⚜

His head pounded. His mouth tasted of the vomit that stained the front of his uniform; the stink filled his nose so that he retched again. His vision was blurred, but it began to clear as he rubbed his eyes. He held his wrist in front of his face. The hands of his watch indicated 0833. "Oh, shit!" he thought. "It's after eight. They'll list me as AWOL. Dammit! Just one more way to screw me."

He looked around. He was in a hangar, but which one? He looked at the airplanes. None of them were T-38s. They were all different, but mostly they were T-39s. He must be in the transient hangar where they parked some of the aircraft visiting the base. The rest would be on the ramp outside. He was lying between two mechanic's chests that contained wrenches and ratchets. He was lying on something so uncomfortable that it seemed to be penetrating the small of his back. Rolling over, he shoved the pair of wire cutters toward the chest on his right.

He couldn't remember how he had gotten to the hangar. He remembered buying two six-packs of beer at the base exchange. He remembered that he needed to call Brenda. "Shit! Brenda!" he said aloud. But coming out through his dried and cracked lips, it sounded more like, "Siiit! Endaaa!" He tasted his vomit and gagged, the back of his throat wanting to come to his lips. Had he talked to her?

Then he remembered. He had called her. She hadn't believed him, but he had the orders. He reached into his fatigue shirt pocket. The folded paper was wet from the vomit, but he unfolded it and read again, "Airman Second Class Thomas Pickerton is ordered to report to Tan San Nhut Air Base, Republic of Vietnam, for duty as a jet engine mechanic." All the rest didn't matter. The bit about getting to Travis AFB, California, the bit about authorized combat pay—none of that was important until you came to the part that read, "This order supersedes Special Order 665478 ordering A/2C Pickerton to Wiesbaden, Germany."

"Assholes! Change my orders. Tell me I can't marry my fiancée, because I'm not a sergeant and I'm going to a combat zone. I mean, fuck! We had it all planned. I'll protest. They can't do this to me."

He was pissed. He had to find the first sergeant. But before that, he'd better get a fresh uniform and shower the vomit out of his hair. He staggered off toward the barracks area. He'd tell them he'd been sick in the night. That he had food poisoning. He'd go to the medical clinic. No, not the medical clinic—they might smell the beer. He'd claim he was so distraught by the new orders that he'd gotten sick. He'd show them the orders. They would believe him. What had Brenda said? That if he didn't want to marry her, he should just say so. Don't blame the air force.

"Well, goddamn it! It's the air force's fault!" he muttered, although it was unintelligible.

⚜

He was still in the fog, but it was not so cold. Perhaps hypothermia was setting in. Wasn't that what they had told him in survival training? Before you freeze, you begin to feel warm, and freezing is like going to sleep. He felt warmth returning, but now he seemed bound, unable to move. The light was still there, brighter than ever, but he still couldn't see through the fog. He kept going on, but now it was more difficult. There seemed to be resistance as he tried to lean forward into the fog. He was still so very tired. He sensed time had passed, but he didn't know how much. He didn't seem to be able to see his watch, but he knew it must be there. He wore it even when he slept, but he couldn't see it now. He tried but couldn't get his arm in front of his face.

"Wait…" His mind paused. "Is that a voice? Relax. Take a deep breath and listen." He tried to expand his chest…he couldn't! Couldn't get his breath! He tried again, but again he could not. His chest moved less than an inch and then stopped. Now he began to feel the pain. It seeped in. It was an itch, then a twitch, then an ache, then a burning sensation, and finally a conflagration of all his muscle, sinew, and bone. He didn't know bones could hurt, but his did. And now even his soul burned as the pain tried to contort his body. But he could not move. Something pressed on his chest. His arms were restricted. His legs felt encased. He could breathe only in short gasps. He was no longer cold. His bones were burning.

"I can't breathe!" He gasped between intakes. "I can't breathe!" The pain was ever increasing. Then, briefly, he saw eyes. They were brown. Just eyes.

Somewhere a voice said, "What are you doing awake? Calm down, Lieutenant. I'm going to give you…" If it was supposed to be soothing, it wasn't. It was more a command, not unlike something he had heard in officer training.

But he couldn't concentrate. He needed to focus, but his eyes would not. Nor would his mind. Neither body nor mind would respond to his will. He wanted the pain to go away, but it would not. He wanted to move, but he could not. Fleetingly, between gasps for breath, he rejected the thought of Dante. This was Milton's lake of fire. Then the fog got heavier. What he thought were voices faded again into the murmur of a distant ocean.

⚜

The barracks were empty, and his roommate was gone. That was good because the room was so small you could barely turn around when both people were there.

The thought struck him that he would be stuck in another barracks in Vietnam. He didn't know if he could take it. He had always been claustrophobic, and the little rooms they expected him to live in made him gasp for air. And as a jet engine mechanic, he had to work every day in freezing-cold, windowless rooms. He suddenly felt closed in, almost to the point of panic. That was why he wanted to go to Germany. He could marry Brenda, and they could have an apartment off the base. He would still have to work in a closed room, but after hours he wouldn't have to be confined, smelling the sweat of others and listening to stupid conversations about women, cars, and sex.

He quickly showered, brushed his teeth, and put on fresh fatigues. He shoved his vomit-stained fatigues under the bottom bunk. He would wash them later.

His hair still wet, he ran back to the flight line, where unusual vehicles were running up and down. Personnel scurried about. It was not the usual choreography of flight launch or recovery.

"Strange," he thought, "there aren't any aircraft in the air." He knew the morning training launches were scheduled for 0630 and there should be aircraft in the pattern and lots of activity as the first launch recovered and the second launch taxied for takeoff. Instead there were fire engines and pickup trucks everywhere. Someone had had an emergency. No one seemed to have missed him.

He saw Harrison and asked him where the first sergeant was.

"Where've you been?" The question was more casual than accusative.

"Ahhh…" His still-clouded mind searched for an excuse. "In the hangar straightening out some tool chests somebody left all messed up. What's going on out here?"

"Geez, man. You must have heard it. I actually saw it. That F-5 that came in yesterday from Cannon—he was leaving this morning. He had a nose-gear problem and tried to come back in. They foamed the runway at five thousand feet, but he never even made it to the foam. Dragged his right wing on touchdown and…geez, man! I've never seen anything like it. He pivoted on his wing, then his nose, then his tail, then his nose, tail, nose—*three times* he cartwheeled it down the runway. He came to a stop just short of the foam."

"Did the pilot die?"

"Don't know. They took him out of the cockpit, and last I heard they were taking him to Wilford Hall over at

Lackland. But that was hours ago. How didn't you hear all the commotion?"

"Oh, I always wear ear protectors, even in the hangar. Don't want to lose my hearing. Shit, man! That's something. Bad day for the pilot. Where's the first sergeant?"

"Uh, he's over at the line-maintenance office, but I wouldn't bother him now. Seems like another of the transient aircraft had a problem and they were going to let it use the T-37 runway on the other side of the base. Then a T-39 taxiing over reported a problem with his gyro. Maintenance thought it might be a loose wire, but when they traced the circuit, it turned out the wire had been cut along with a bunch of others. So the first sergeant's supervising a look at all the other aircraft parked in the transient area. He's kind of pissed. I wouldn't mess with him right now."

"But, man…I have to see him. He has to do something about these orders."

"Oh yeah. Well, congrats. I heard you got Germany. That's great."

"No, man. The fucking air force changed the orders to Tan San Nhut yesterday. I got to see the first sergeant about getting them changed back."

"Bummer, man! Too bad. Well, like I said, he's over in the line-maintenance office. Good luck."

As Pickerton entered the maintenance office, the first sergeant was yelling orders over the FM radio set. He almost screamed as he told this unit and that to get over to such-and-such airplane.

"We think we've narrowed it to the nose-well areas. Check the wiring in the nose wells. Look at every single airplane on the line. T-38s, transients, everything!"

The first sergeant turned to the base commander. "T-37 flight line is shutting down, sir. All aircraft aloft are being recalled and given straight-in landing instructions. All aircraft on the ground are being checked."

"How many so far?" the base commander asked.

"Eight, sir. I suspect that when they examine the wreckage of Aggressor oh-nine, they'll find wires cut in the nose wheel well. Probably the wires to the shimmy damper on the nose gear and the worm-gear activator for locking the wing gear in place. That would account for both the stuck nose gear and the failure of the right main on touchdown. Do we know anything about the pilot?"

"He's in surgery and will be for some time. I don't know the details, but he's in pretty bad shape."

The base commander asked for the list of aircraft on which inspections had found the damaged wires and, using his walkie-talkie, asked his executive officer to contact the wing commander's office and set up a briefing so he could bring him up to date. As he spoke, three individuals in plainclothes entered the office. Each wore on the chest pocket of his suit coat the badge of the Air Force Office of Special Investigations—OSI. "On whose authority are these guys here?" the base commander asked himself.

The OSI officers immediately began questioning the first sergeant, who held up his hand commanding them to stop and then, with the same hand, pointed to the base commander. The special agents turned and surrounded the senior officer.

⚜

The burning had stopped, and while he sensed that his feet were once again freezing cold, the rest of his body seemed not to exist. He continued to hear the murmurings, and once or twice he felt as if the earth moved under him. It was almost as if a large animal were walking nearby. There was a thump, and he shook; a wait, another thump, and he shook again. But always there was the fog. The fog through which he could not see, the fog that distorted sound, the fog that had borne with it freezing cold and insufferable heat and pain.

No longer did he have a sense of time or place. Even being was questionable. If he could not see or hear, did he exist? "I think, therefore I am" passed through his mind like a branch carried by a flooded stream. He could not concentrate, but he was aware. Was that thinking? Did that qualify as existence? Attempts to capture and dwell on complete thoughts failed. It was as if he were sitting in a theater watching a feature-length presentation of a film made up of one or two frames from each of thousands of completely disassociated movies.

"God," he wondered. "Where is God?" Images of Bible stories flashed through his mind. Moses on Sinai, Jesus on the cross, the Red Sea parting, Jesus looking down on the world with the devil. Too fast. They went too fast, but they differed from the other images. These were in color. Then back into monochrome—where images continued to streak through his mind. Mr. Chips, Dreyfus, Robert Jordan, Jake Barnes, Frankie in his iron lung, an unknown cripple on crutches. All sped away but left their traces—not on his mind but on his soul. He felt as if his heart would ache if he could but feel it. Still, his soul felt, and it ached.

⚜

Pickerton, thinking it best not to bother the first sergeant at that particular moment, reported to his line chief, who put him to work going through parked aircraft, looking for wires that had been cut. He pulled the nose-gear door downward and wedged his head and upper torso into the wheel well. Awkwardly, he brought his flashlight up while his free hand searched for anything that looked out of place. He found nothing on the first aircraft or the second. His third aircraft was a T-39 parked at the end of the transient parking area. It had been ignored by earlier inspectors because it had an engine cowling open and there were engine stands next to it.

Looking up into the well, he noticed a yellow wire that bowed out from its bundle. Reaching up, he pulled gently on it, and it came away from the bundle. The end of the wire had definitely been cut. He tugged gently on other wires in the bundle, and three more came out.

Extracting himself from the wheel well, he called out, "Over here! I've got some cut wires."

His line chief and four or five other mechanics arrived on the run. The line chief edged his way into the nose well to look and, pulling out, said, "Yep, same as the others. Not just cut but stuck back into the bundle so that a cursory inspection wouldn't detect any damage. Son of a bitch knew what he was doing. He didn't intend for any of these things to be found on the ground. We were lucky, I guess, about that T-39 gyro."

"Well, not everybody was lucky," interjected one of the sergeants. "How about the pilot of Aggressor oh-nine?"

"Well, except him," the line chief answered. "But it could have been a whole lot worse if these other aircraft had gotten airborne."

⚜

The pain had returned. Not like before, but enough. It taunted him, almost as if it were daring him to move or think about it. The bright overhead sun had gone away, and the murmurs had become voices once more. He tried to turn his head to see who spoke, but could not. He tried to lift his arm in front of his face to look at his watch, but could not. He still found himself breathing in short gasps and trying not to panic because he could not draw a deep breath.

He was still very tired and drifted in and out of consciousness. Each time he woke, his eyes focused just a little better. He tried to talk but felt as if his mouth were full of sand. He was terribly thirsty. Never had he been thirstier. It was a new and uncomfortable experience. But then, so was the pain.

No longer did images rush through his mind. He could think coherently enough but still had no answers and very few clues. The ceiling was asbestos tile with thousands of little holes. It was semidark, or was it semilight? The voices were voices, but they remained unintelligible. There was a door—he could tell because the light changed as it opened and closed. He could see the shadow the door cast on the ceiling.

He tried to speak, but his lips seemed not to move at his command. A grunt emerged from his throat. More eyes peered down at him. They were clearer now. There was a mask—a surgical mask—below the eyes. It spoke:

"Lieutenant Thibodeaux, welcome back. We thought you might have wandered away from us, but you're going to be fine."

The voice faded, and the eyes seemed to recede into a long tunnel through which he was moving backward with ever-increasing speed. As the tunnel grew longer and longer, he felt time passing. The tunnel was time; it must be. He was moving through time, stopping occasionally at stations along the way only long enough for a pair of eyes above a mask to speak to him briefly. Still, each time they confirmed to him that he continued to exist.

The pain seemed to recede as he whizzed through the tunnel but grow stronger the nearer he came to each stop. Anticipating the stops, he tried hard to ignore the pain. He wanted—no, needed—to speak with the mask and the eyes.

He needed information, but the pain kept him from speaking. And then he left the station again, moving backward, increasing his speed through time.

⚜

"They're definitely your fingerprints, Airman Pickerton. We found vomit on the floor and vomit on the fatigue uniform under your bunk. We found your wire cutters near the vomit in the hangar. They have only your fingerprints on them. There are beer bottles behind the tool chests. They have your fingerprints as well. Would you like to tell us what happened?"

"I don't know what happened. I remember talking to Brenda. She yelled at me and accused me of having the air force change my orders so I wouldn't have to marry her. I remember going to the hangar to have a beer because alcohol isn't allowed in the barracks and I can't stand being confined in that shoebox they call a semiprivate room. It isn't big enough for one person, and it doesn't have a window. It's just a closet really, but so are all the other so-called rooms in the barracks." He almost spit when he said "rooms."

"Then I woke up, looked at my watch, and realized I was late for duty. I went back to the barracks, took a shower, put on some clean fatigues, and reported to the flight line. I had to see the first sergeant about getting my orders changed. That's it. Maybe somebody came in and gave me the wire cutters or put them under me while I was asleep. Honest! I don't remember anything else." He tried to rise from the chair, but the OSI agent grabbed him by the shoulder and forced him back down.

Another agent knocked on the door, entered, and handed the special agent in charge a piece of paper.

"Well, I'm sorry, Airman, but your fingerprints were found all over the wheel wells and gear doors of all the aircraft where we found cut wires. The air force will provide you a lawyer."

Turning to the agent who had just entered, the special agent said, "Tell the JAG we'll be ready for an Article Thirty-Two hearing this afternoon."

⚜

"How long?"

"What?"

"How long?"

"If you mean how long have you been here, the answer is three weeks."

"Three weeks? How could it be just three weeks? It seems like decades—or maybe eons. I thought I passed through centuries in the tunnel." He mumbled almost incoherently but not so badly the doctor didn't know what he was saying.

"Yes, morphine can do that to you. But it's only three weeks."

"Only three weeks," Thibodeaux said weakly. "Only three weeks."

The doctor was standing above him. There was no mask now. The face seemed older, but to Thibodeaux, at the age of twenty-two, most faces seemed older. The hair was salt and pepper. The eyes were not brown but blue green. These were not the eyes he had seen before, nor was the voice the one that had greeted him at many of the stations along the tunnel.

The doctor was shining a light from a small pen into his eyes. He wanted Thibodeaux to follow the light with his eyes. Having learned just last night that his eyes were the only part of his body—other than his lips—that could move, he tracked the light as if it were his intended target in an air-combat engagement.

Fighting against the constant pressure under his chin, he spoke through gritted teeth. "How long before I can return to flying?"

"Flying?" The doctor's voice carried a certain incredulity. "I think you had better think about sitting up before you consider flying."

Not one for dwelling on what he couldn't do, Thibodeaux started to explain to the doctor what a waste it would be if the top graduate in his pilot-training class—the one with the highest scores *ever* in undergraduate pilot training—did not return to the cockpit. At that moment, however, technicians arrived with a device to go behind the bed, and the doctor was required to move.

It was a mirror that slanted forward. Now Thibodeaux could see to the foot of the bed and beyond. Although he had no significant peripheral vision because the cast encased the sides of his head, his field of vision was no longer restricted to just the ceiling tiles. He looked again, constructing a larger image by extrapolating from what he saw and what he perceived with his hearing. There was no bed across from him, but he sensed a bed to his right. The edge of a doorjamb was visible at the extreme left of the mirror, so he knew there was a door to his left. Yes, he knew everything was reversed in the mirror—but not in its relation to his bed or his head.

He had no wife or family in Texas, so there was no one to come and describe for him other things. He would have to coax nurses and orderlies into taking time to describe his surroundings. He knew his father and mother were there somewhere, but he wouldn't want them to remain at his side. He was alive, and things would be what they would be. He had to master these challenges himself, and he certainly didn't want to talk to his father about returning to Mobile and entering the family business. Not now.

He could see himself in the lower part of the mirror by cutting his eyes upward. His face retained traces of bruising with purplish-black patches of blood not yet absorbed. His head was held in a plaster collar that extended up beyond his ears, and the constant pressure under his chin was part of a harness that disappeared somewhere north of his head. He was obviously in traction. The plaster cast extended downward, shrouding his entire body, including both shoulders.

He could feel air moving across his left forearm, and he could move that appendage slightly, flexing the fingers in his hand. But he could not move the upper arm at all. His right arm was immobilized, covered to his fingertips in plaster. He could feel the plaster on his right leg, and now could see it went all the way to his toes. His couldn't move his left leg, but it didn't seem to have any plaster on it. Thinking about it, he realized there were probably weights on both legs if he was actually in traction, and it appeared he was.

Well, at least he could see to the door using the new mirror. He tried to be casual—even jocular—but the image he could now see frightened him. It was as if a cold black shadow passed through his soul. In his mind all he could see was Frankie in his iron lung, trying to joke as he looked backward through his mirror. He hadn't spoken to Frankie since visiting him in that hospital; the family had moved away, and when they went back to visit, no one in the hospital could—or perhaps would—tell him anything about Frankie. Would that happen to him?

⚜

"It's a real waste, you know," the first sergeant said to his collected minions. "He was a really good jet mechanic. You know, she not only didn't come to his court martial; she refused to read his letters. She sent them all back unopened."

"Yeah," the team lead said. "She's a real bitch. You know he had a year of college before he joined? He enlisted because he wanted to marry her and it was the fastest way to get an income. So he gives up college to marry her, and then she stiffs him when this happens. He may have been a pretty smart guy otherwise, but his decisions about women were pretty bad."

"Pretty smart guys don't get drunk and cut wiring bundles on air force aircraft and then not remember what they did," the first sergeant observed.

"So what happens to him now?" asked one of the mechanics.

"Leavenworth," the first sergeant answered. "That's where they send all the long-term military prisoners."

"Twenty years is a long time."

"Yeah, but he's only twenty-one now, so he'll just be forty-one when he comes out. Age-wise it's like serving twenty in the air force and then retiring," the team lead mused.

"True," said the first sergeant. "But when he 'retires,' he'll have a criminal record and a dishonorable discharge to overcome. It'll be tough. You know, though, he might be out in fifteen years if they give him parole. Maybe even ten."

Everyone agreed it was a tragedy and went back to work. The break was over.

⚜

Having no knowledge of what other people thought about him, Pickerton regarded himself as a betrayed lover, and more, as a betrayed loyalist. Even his parents had disowned his behavior. Good boy gone bad. They blamed the girl. They had never liked her all through high school. They were sure she would tell him she was pregnant to get him to marry her. And even though that hadn't happened, when he dropped out of college to join the air force, they knew it was only a matter of time before other bad things happened. Their anger only fed his anger. Although in the back of his mind, he knew he alone was responsible, he could not yet admit it to himself. He used self-pity to defend himself against the stares and innuendoes of others while they processed him through the various levels of military discipline until he was escorted into a cell at Fort Leavenworth Federal Prison. The windowless box was six feet wide and ten feet long. It held a narrow bunk and a toilet. That was it. There was one shelf above the bunk. Rather than bars along the front—as he had seen in prisons in the movies—there was a solid-steel door that had a reverse peephole and a sliding partition through which he could receive trays or books or, if necessary, place his hands for handcuffs.

He would remain in this cell until authorities moved him to a different section of the prison so he could interact with some of the other prisoners. They thought he might be at risk because the normal thieves and murderers in Leavenworth took a dim view of spies and saboteurs. He was there because he had been charged with, and had pled guilty to, sabotage of government equipment. It would take time before he was accepted into the general population. If ever.

The first night he felt as if he could not move. It was as if the ceiling were pressing on his chest. It was darker than he feared. No light found its way into the cell. He found breathing difficult. The walls restricted him on all sides. His breath came in gasps. He wanted to claw his way out, but he could not. They had buried him alive. If he did not die, surely he would go crazy. He would appeal! This was torture, and they weren't allowed to torture him. It was that thought that helped him through the night, and the light was turned on the next day. At least he thought it was the next day. Already he had lost track of time.

⚜

"Good morning, Lieutenant, sir!" A cheerful voice if ever he had heard one. Standing at the foot of the bed was an individual in blue regulation hospital pajama pants and a blue-and-white seersucker robe. He was leaning on two crutches. He was young, with dark hair cut in regulation style, although a wayward lock kept falling over his left eyebrow. Above his broad smile were two dark, extremely bright eyes. Hanging from his shoulder and across his body was what appeared to be a newsboy's canvas bag.

"Airman First Class Fowler at your service. You need, I fetch. Something to read today?"

Through his clenched teeth, Thibodeaux responded. "Not quite sure how I would hold a book. Little encumbered at the moment."

"Uh, what was that, sir? It's a little difficult to understand you. Just a minute."

The man maneuvered his crutches and almost immediately stood leaning over Thibodeaux's face. This close he looked even younger. Thibodeaux wondered if he was even shaving yet.

"OK, sir, let's try that again."

"I said, I don't think I can handle a book," Thibodeaux grunted, the traction strap under his chin keeping his teeth closed.

"Oh, that's no problem, sir. I also read. So if there's something you want to hear, I can give you half an hour in the morning and maybe a little less in the evening. I'll have to check my schedule book." With that, he drew a small black book from his bag. "Yes, sir. Half an hour in the mornings, and I can pencil you in for some time each evening when they take Captain Komenda to hydrotherapy."

"What day is it?" Thibodeaux grunted.

"Tuesday, sir. We'll have turkey soup and rice on the lunch trays."

"No, what's the date?"

"Does it really matter, sir? The date is only relative to those on the outside. For those of us in here, it's Tuesday, and we'll get turkey soup and some banana pudding."

Strangely, Thibodeaux understood.

"Say, sir, I hear you stayed on the bull, but it landed on you."

"What?"

"Just a figure of speech, sir. I'm from Wyoming, where we ride bulls in rodeos. Sometimes a cowboy stays on the bull, but the bull falls on him, and the cowboy gets injured. Way they tell the story, you stayed on the bull, but it fell on you."

Thibodeaux thought about it a moment. "Yes, I guess that's so. Sometimes you do everything right, and the bull falls on you."

Fowler smiled. "That's good, Lieutenant. Glad to see you don't feel sorry for yourself. Too many guys in here do, you know. Like that major down the hall. There's no getting that guy out of the wallow he's made for himself. Couple of broken legs is all, and you'd think he was dying. I guess his problem is that everybody else up here is aircraft related and his was a car wreck. And, confidentially, I hear he was drunk when he did it. So now he's here with all these hero types, and he doesn't know what to do, so he sulks and complains about being put in with junior officers and enlisted men."

Thibodeaux listened but quickly grunted, "Fowler, I'm not sure I'd go around telling stories, especially about field-grade officers. Might get you in trouble. I mean, what if I told somebody what you said?"

"Right, sure, sir. I understand, but, I mean, what are they going to do? Put me in a helicopter and send me to Vietnam? Been there, done that, got the T-shirt." At this he pulled his robe open, displaying a green T-shirt with a green hornet silk-screened on it. Around the hornet was printed in gold, "20th Special Operations Squadron—Green Hornets."

Closing the robe, he continued. "Besides, sir, how else are you going to have anything to think about if I don't keep you up on all the scuttlebutt? After all, I'm the only ambulatory person on this ward. So listen, there's a nice little library on the second floor. What can I get you to read—as in, what can I get to read *to* you?"

"How about today's paper?" Thibodeaux growled through his teeth.

"No, sir, no paper reading. I don't like reading news, and you won't like hearing it. Just makes you irritated. No, sir. Philosophy, theology, engineering, murder, mayhem, but no news. Not good for your healing process."

"So now you're a doctor?"

"Oh, no, sir. Wouldn't ever want to be a doctor. It's way too sad a profession for me. I just want to go back to Wyoming and raise horses. But if I've learned nothing else in my short air force career, it's that worrying about things over which you have no control doesn't do you, or those around you, any good. It's like, why would you go and poke a stick at a nest of rattlesnakes? You're better off ignoring them and getting the hell out of the area."

"OK, so no newspapers," Thibodeaux grunted. "What do you suggest?"

"Well sir, Captain Komenda is reading this book on philosophy by Michel de Montaigne. I'm learning a lot from it. Mostly it's just common sense, but, like, you never think about it. Sure helps a lot for people who don't get out much. Then there's this fellow Camus. We read him last month. He's got an interesting take on life. Doesn't believe in God, he says, but somehow I'm not really convinced. He has a lot to say because he was in a sanatorium for TB for a good amount of time. He didn't get around much, kind of like you. Of course there's always Agatha Christie or one of the other crime and mystery writers. Pick your poison." He laughed at his joke. Thibodeaux got it but only groaned.

"So who's Captain Komenda?" Thibodeaux asked.

"He's my pilot. We were crew on Green Hornet Thirty-Five. He was the aircraft commander, Lieutenant Mead was the co-pilot, and I was the crew chief and door gunner. That's how we ended up in here. We got shot down up by Thuy Wah while attacking what we thought was a small fuel dump. Turned out to be a truck park with multiple ZSU-23s defending it. Lieutenant Mead didn't make it. I got this." He gestured with his head toward his right leg.

"Captain Komenda took the stick in his head and crushed the front part of his skull. He also broke his back. They put a plate in his head and fused his spine, and now they're teaching him to walk again. He swears he'll fly again, but I don't know." Fowler shifted himself on his crutches, easing the plastered leg to a more comfortable position. "Every time they take him outside, he has terrible headaches from the cold affecting the plate in his head. He says it just takes some getting used to, and willpower. Captain Komenda is a great believer in willpower. Anyway, he's my pilot, so I have to take care of him. Might as well do what I can for everybody else who's up here while I'm at it. It's not like you guys can run down to the library on your own. These crutches make me mobile, and I can maneuver on them about as well as I can walk in a pair of boots with riding heels." To demonstrate he pirouetted on one crutch, catching himself with the second and swinging back into a position next to the bed. This, of course, went completely unnoticed by Thibodeaux, who lost sight of Fowler the moment he quit bending over the head of the bed.

"So then, do we call you Mercury or Hermes?" Thibodeaux asked.

"Mercury or Hermes?" Fowler's voice rose in a question at the end.

"Sure. Hermes was the Greek messenger of the gods, and Mercury was what the Romans called him. Obviously the reading you and Captain Komenda have been doing hasn't included mythology."

"Say, isn't there a tie made by somebody called Hermes?" Fowler asked, somewhat unsure of himself.

"Absolutely. Hermes is a big Parisian haute couture place. Ties, scarves, purses, jackets—everything a well-dressed lady or gentleman could need as an accoutrement." Thibodeaux's French sounded less like a practiced second language and more like the noise a rutting pig makes. Although his grunted English was understandable, his clenched-teeth French sounded like German or something Slavic. But Fowler got the idea.

"Well, I guess we better go with Mercury. I think I'd rather be known by the name of a high-class Ford than some polka-dot tie."

"OK, well then, Mercury, I'll listen to whatever you want to read. Now fly off to wherever it is you have to be."

Thibodeaux was tired. This was the most he had talked since waking from the surgeries. The pain was getting worse, but he knew they would come with the morphine in a little while. His awareness of the morphine bothered him. Perhaps he should have more willpower and less morphine. Maybe

Captain Komenda was right. Well, he would give it some thought—maybe lots of thought. He had the time.

Fowler swung off, and Thibodeaux saw in his mirror the bottoms of the crutches and his heels as he cleared the door. "Heels," thought Thibodeaux. "How appropriate. But he uses crutches instead of wings."

⚜

And so they read and talked. Fowler was there promptly each morning, his book in the bag. He would place himself in a leaning position over Thibodeaux's left shoulder, wedged between the bed frame and the wall so that both his hands were free to hold the book. He would read, stopping often to discuss this passage or that thought. In addition, he offered stories about Wyoming or what he would do when he collected all the back pay the air force owed him. He told Thibodeaux what the weather was like outside and how lucky they were to be inside, and always he talked about how Captain Komenda was doing. Of course, Thibodeaux had never met Komenda—or, for that matter, any of the other denizens of the orthopedic floor—but he knew about each one in detail through Mercury's uncanny narrative ability. He knew about those who left and those who came. Only once did one of them, a captain in a wheelchair, stop by on his way out to whatever the world had become since Thibodeaux had been confined.

"Been hearing from Fowler for weeks there was a baby fighter pilot up here." His chair was at the foot of Thibodeaux's bed. He couldn't have been more than thirty, but he looked seventy. His face was thin and worn. His eyes betrayed a man who had experienced a great deal of pain. He was wearing a leather contraption that encircled his waist and from which emanated ascending metal spokes that curved back in at his neck. His head was held upright and rigid by the brace that encircled his head at the chin and under the ears.

"Now that they're sending me home on convalescent leave, thought I'd stop by for a personal reconnaissance. Johnson, F-105s. Thirty-Sixth Fighter Squadron out of Korat. Lost a race with a SAM over northern Laos and punched out. Broke my blasted back. Going too fast when I pulled the handles."

By now able to be heard through his teeth at a distance greater than a foot or so, Thibodeaux answered, "Thibodeaux, F-5s. First Aggressors out of Cannon. Gear collapsed. Sabotage, they tell me. Guess I broke my back as well. Neck, shoulder, leg—name it, it's broken. Hell, I think I broke my tailbone." He forced what he hoped sounded like a laugh.

"Well, I'd like to stay and swap lies, but you'd be at a disadvantage since you can't use your hands—and besides, my family is waiting on me downstairs." The captain paused, then continued.

"Thibodeaux, I know we fighter pilots are all pretty tough guys and don't take advice very well, but let me give you some anyway. From what I hear, you're a pretty good guy. Smart and well grounded. Remember that when they come to change that cast. Remember it when they start your rehabilitation. Find your center. Concentrate. That roller coaster ride you took down the runway is going to seem like Disneyland compared to what's coming. If you think your instructors in pilot training were sadistic bastards, wait till you meet your physical therapists. But remember, just like the instructors, they'll make you better. Keep putting in the corrective control responses in the proper sequence, and eventually she'll come out of the spin. If she doesn't…well, you're dead, and then you don't care anyway. *Ding hao*, Lieutenant."

"Thanks, I think" was all Thibodeaux could muster in reply. But as the captain's wheelchair was disappearing from the mirror's edge, Thibodeaux grunted, "Fly safe!"

The next morning, cheerful as ever, Fowler was there with more stories about who was being done unto on the ward.

"Why don't you go home?" Thibodeaux blurted the question completely out of the blue. In fact, it was like an attack out of the sun. Fowler never saw it coming. Thibodeaux had him in his sights and raked him nose to tail. Thibodeaux felt miserable the moment he asked. It was kind of like attacking some flier who had just dropped his gear to surrender.

"I'm sorry. Did you want me to leave?"

"No, I don't want you to leave. I want to know why you stay around so many miserable people. I want to know how you can be so goddamn cheerful. I want to know why you don't go home to Wyoming and be with your family."

"Well, aren't we in a mood this morning?" Fowler replied. "Gee, Lieutenant, I didn't know I got on your nerves so badly."

"Fowler, you don't get on my nerves. You're the one ray of sunshine in this otherwise stygian world, but I honestly feel guilty if—in even a small way—I'm keeping you in this place."

"Lieutenant, you're not keeping me here. Captain Komenda isn't keeping me here. The doctors aren't keeping me here. I stay here because this is where my family is. In Wyoming, I've got a father who drinks but means well. He works on somebody else's ranch. My mother remarried a sheep farmer, and they barely get by. For either one of them, having me move in would be a burden. I tried it for a week. I couldn't work, and having to take care of me only meant they had to give up something else they needed to be doing, just to make it all come out even. I mean, can you see me riding a horse or roping a stray? Yeeehi! Git along, little dogie!" He slapped his leg cast with his hand.

"You know what we do in Wyoming when a horse breaks his leg? We shoot him. We shoot him because he isn't going to be of any use. All he'll do is take up stable space and eat the oats and hay that a productive horse could be using. Hell, sir, I can't even stock the shelves in a 7-Eleven.

"No, sir. This hospital is where my family is. Captain Komenda is like an older brother. He needs me. Hell, even you need me. Besides, on this ward, he who can move, commands. I'm the only one who can get around, so I'm not just an equal here—I'm a superior. Works out for just about everybody, wouldn't you say? Now, do you want to hear what's happened to that major down the hall with the broken legs?"

⚜

"It really isn't fair," he thought. "I'm paying for something I have absolutely no memory of doing. Something so far from my nature that I myself am disgusted by it." His breathing rate increased.

The cell seemed to close in on him. In the months he had been incarcerated, he had noticed that the more distressed or agitated he became, the smaller the cell became. It became more difficult to breathe. During these episodes he could feel the cell move. It didn't collapse; it just moved, almost stealthily. He could swear it pinned him to the bunk. He was unable to rise, unable even to turn over. It pressed in on him. His breath came in gasps. He couldn't take a full breath. He panicked. He wanted to call out but could not. He tried to calm himself by concentrating on taking slower breaths, by telling himself it was all in his mind, that he was in no danger. Slowly the walls seemed to recede. His breathing returned to normal.

He must gain control of himself. It would, he thought, take time, but he had twenty years—no, less than that now. He could do it. His discussions with the prison psychologist and chaplain were helping. He knew he had to learn not to allow his emotions to drive his perceptions. He needed to become detached and objective. He had talked to the psychologist about self-hypnosis. He wondered if the prison library had any books about it. Maybe his parents could send him the books. He would study and learn to control himself. Wasn't it, after all, lack of control that had gotten him here? Maybe the psychologist could help him find ways to do it.

At the urging of the psychologist, he wrote his parents, again apologizing for his actions and the embarrassment he had caused himself and the family. This time he explained his thinking about control and asked them to see if they could arrange for him to get some books on self-hypnosis. What else, then, did he need to do? He had apologized to his parents. Apologized to the air force and his unit. Perhaps he should apologize to that pilot who had been hurt. He didn't know how to get in touch with him. Maybe his parents or the prison chaplain could find out. What would he say in the letter? "I'm sorry"? Sounded more than a little lame. He could explain about Brenda…but that was just an excuse. Still, it was the truth, and wasn't there something about the truth setting you free? He would talk to the chaplain about how to write the letter, but first, maybe if he just tried…

He took his pencil and wrote, "Dear Lieutenant Thibodeaux…"

⚜

Like a piece of furniture, Thibodeaux lay there. He wondered that people didn't set coffee cups or glasses on him. His head was hidden by the plaster that extended, like the metal neck of an armored suit, up his neck to the top of his head. His feet were covered with a thin blanket of air force blue. His right arm was thrown outward, the cast extending to his fingertips. The left arm exited the plaster at his biceps, but it was pinned to the side of his body with tubes in the veins. The plaster of the body cast went down to his crotch. He might as well be a coffee table or a credenza. Sure, they checked on him every so often, but most of the time he just lay there, listening and looking into his overhead mirror at the foreshortened or elongated forms of people as they moved into and away from the focal point. People pretty much forgot he was there.

Thus it had been that Thursday. He knew it was Thursday because he had smelled the chicken soup on the cart as they wheeled it by. Thursday of some week after he had been there—how long? Still, as Fowler had predicted, weeks had become unimportant. It could have been months. He had little idea of time other than it was Thursday, definitely Thursday, because they had chicken soup. Two doctors had stopped at the door to the ward, unaware of their eavesdropper.

"Yes, but when are you going to tell him? He deserves to know." The first doctor spoke quietly.

"I don't know. I mean, I hate this part of the business. It sucks big-time. I suppose I'll tell him when it becomes more obvious."

"Before you move him up to the seventh floor, I hope."

"Of course before I move him there. Everybody in the hospital knows that's hospice. Geez! I'm not so unfeeling that I would spring it on him and move him up all at the same time. I just want him to enjoy the little time he has left."

"Why don't you discharge him and let him go home? Isn't that what we do with ambulatory patients?"

"Dammit! I did that. He went home and came back a week later. He didn't want to be home. He wanted to be here, so I let him stay. I had him admitted as a cancer patient without his knowledge. He thinks he's back on the orthopedic floor."

"Well, all I can say is it's a damn shame. Damned fine kid, hero and all that. Did you hear they want to give him the Air Force Cross? Seems that when he and Komenda were shot down, he pulled Komenda out of the burning aircraft even with that shattered right leg. He tried to get the copilot as well, but he was already dead. Then he took his M-16 and held a bunch of North Vietnamese regulars at bay until the other helicopters could get in to rescue them. If he was an officer, I think they'd be giving him a Medal of Honor."

"Yes, I know all about that. He specifically said he didn't want the ceremony until after he's out of his cast and off his crutches. It has something to do with returning to duty with Captain Komenda. And I suspect that's why he's back here. He's developed some sort of attachment to the captain and feels only he can take care of him. I've really never seen anything quite like it."

"Well, we both know Komenda isn't going back on active duty, so that's a nonstarter."

"Yes, and I think even Fowler knows that, but he isn't going to tell Komenda. It's a strange bond, but I think it does Komenda a world of good, and Lord knows it's given Fowler a purpose. So as far as I'm concerned, we aren't going to meddle until we have to."

"Well, I agree with you: the whole thing sucks. We put nineteen pieces of bone back together to give him his leg only to discover bone cancer. Dammit! Sometimes I hate what we do."

The doctors moved away, but Thibodeaux now bore a secret that weighed on his heart so heavily he literally shrank within his cast. It wasn't just the muscle atrophy he was experiencing; somehow he felt himself physically diminished and morally exhausted.

⚜

Pickerton concentrated on his breathing. Letting go of his fear, he allowed it to fall as if from a great height. A height so remote that he lost sight of the fear as it fell to whatever was below. He sought to empty himself of thought. He could feel his heart beat. He sensed the pulsing of blood through his arteries and veins. It moved in waves, and each wave took him deeper into the aura of energy that surrounded him. He could exist like this forever, but what was forever? Time had no meaning for him. Today, yesterday, tomorrow—all were the same. For yesterday had been now, today was now, and tomorrow would become now. *Now* was important, and *now* he felt there was no need to control, no need to fear. There was only a need to be and, in being, to allow all around him to be unto itself.

Still, there were things he understood that the "now" demanded if he were to honor the concept. He roused himself to once again attempt the letter to the lieutenant. Each time he tried, guilt rushed out of the void and crushed him under its weight. His breathing again came in gasps, and the walls began to slide downward and in. Yet each start gave him hope that one day he would be able to do it. He could not forgive himself until he sought forgiveness from the lieutenant. Both the chaplain and the psychologist agreed. He must cast out that final demon before he could achieve peace and before he could hope to begin a true rebuilding of his life. Once again he tried. "Dear Lieutenant Thibodeaux..."

⚜

Thibodeaux attempted joviality when Fowler came to read. He called him Quick Silver, although in his mind he thought more of Hephaestus, the lame god misbegotten of Hera and Zeus. Still, Thibodeaux attempted humor. Fowler, he of uncanny ability, saw through it immediately. At first Fowler thought it a recurrence of the guilt Thibodeaux had earlier expressed about Fowler staying in the hospital, but he quickly realized it was something deeper than that.

"OK, Lieutenant. I don't know how you found out, since I know you can't get out of that bed, but out with it. You know, don't you?"

"Know what?"

"You know about my cancer."

"What cancer?"

"Lieutenant, you're not a good liar. You're not even a passable liar. You *know*."

"Hell, Fowler. I don't want to know. I didn't want to know. But when you're a log on the beach, all kinds of things happen to you. I'm really sorry. I didn't know you knew. In fact, I understood they hadn't told you."

"Told me? Listen, Lieutenant. Nurses and doctors come to *me* when they want to know what's happening on this ward. Heck, I knew the day they readmitted me. They sent me for a blood test, and the tech was all apologies. Wanted to know if it hurt much and that sort of thing. That they didn't tell me about the cancer, and that they didn't suggest a treatment, that tells me everything else I need to know."

"But how do you do it?"

"Do what?"

"Stay so damned happy?"

"What's the alternative, sir? Do you want me to check in to the seventh floor and sit around moaning about dying?"

"But, Robert, I still don't understand." Thibodeaux used Fowler's Christian name for the first time in their exchanges.

"Lieutenant." Fowler never used first names, always ranks. "You know when we first met and I told you me and Captain Komenda were reading Montaigne? I told you Montaigne had a philosophy that was pretty much just common sense. Well, one thing he says is 'Unable to govern events, I govern myself.' Now that's the key, see? Everyone is responsible for himself. Now that guy Camus says that even if there is no God and no heaven or hell, we need to find a purpose in life. A purpose that is worthy of our life, since there's not going to be anything else. It's all pretty simple, really. See, heaven is this place we make ourselves. So is hell. And we're, like, walking on a beam suspended between the two. It's up to us as individuals whether we jump off on the heaven side or fall off on the hell side. Still, I sometimes think about whether there really is a God. What do you think, sir? Is there a God?"

Unable to brush the tears from his eyes, Thibodeaux blinked several times to clear his vision and sniffed to unstop his nose. All of this was difficult with the chin strap pulling his mouth closed.

"A God? I just turned twenty-three. How the hell would I know? I haven't got enough experience to tell you if the Taj Mahal is really white or if draining water spins the opposite way in Australia. But yes, Fowler, I think there is a God. At this moment, he's not on my list of close friends. In fact, I think he's pretty much a son of a bitch. But yes, he—or she, or it—is there. If I thought I'd be happier in the world by denying him, I would do it. I have absolutely no idea how he applies to any of this, because God is an infinite concept and I am a finite being. When I try to understand the infinite with my finite mind, it only confuses me and makes my head hurt, so I guess your philosophy is the best we can do. But I'm really sorry, Robert. Really sorry."

"It's OK, sir. I'm not sorry. I've got a really good life. You couldn't ask for more. Friends, being needed, being useful, people who will remember me—isn't that what we all want? Isn't it all we really need? Don't feel sorry for me, sir. I'm one of the lucky ones. I found a philosophy that works, and I'm smart enough to know it. I just hope this bad leg doesn't give way when I go to jump off the beam." He smiled.

"Oh, before I forget, there was a letter for you at the nurses' station. I have it in my bag. Would you like me to read it?"

"Sure, whatever. It's probably from my mother."

"No, sir, I don't think it's from your mother," Fowler said as he ripped the end from the envelope.

"'Dear Lieutenant Thibodeaux...'"

⚜

And so it went, each man balancing himself on the narrow beam he must traverse, suspended somewhere between heaven and hell.

---

"Between Heaven and Hell" originally appeared as the prologue to the author's second novel, *Flying Blind*.

# A December Rain

⚜

The sky was definitely becoming overcast as he pedaled homeward. He wondered if tomorrow would be a wet throw. He might get lucky, though, and have it blow through today. He would watch the six o'clock weather report on TV tonight, but they hardly ever got it right.

There would be no morning paper on Christmas, so he got that day off, as well as New Year's Day. He pitied the poor slobs who threw the afternoon paper, because they would have to deliver on the holiday. But Christmas was still a week away, and he would have to throw every day until then.

His hands were freezing. Although it hardly ever got cold enough on the Gulf Coast for him to wear gloves, this year the weather had been more like stuff that happened up North.

His only experience with going north had been a year ago, when he had accompanied his father on a business trip to New York City. The train took two full days to get there, and then he and his father had to stand outside Pennsylvania Station forever before they could catch a taxi for the hotel. He thought he would never be warm again. The restaurant that evening had seemed like heaven.

Well, heaven this morning would be the living room of his house. It was certainly cold enough for a fire in the fireplace, and he hoped his father had one going. They had used his uncle's pickup truck to bring wood all the way down from his grandfather's farm in northern Mississippi. There was hickory, oak, some poplar, and some really good smelling cedar. A little pine also gave the room a festive smell. He liked the way it scented the room.

They had put the Christmas tree up in the corner of the living room, and its smell had begun to creep through to the dining room and hallway. With a stick or two of pine on the fire, very nice! All in all, it was turning into an OK Christmastime. His brother and sister were doing their best to help out, so with a little luck they'd have a nice Christmas. He wasn't sure why, but he had a feeling this needed to be a good holiday.

As he passed the house, he could see they were going to need some paint on the side in the spring. The two-story house stretched out over the entire lot, its front just a few feet off the sidewalk and its back just a couple of yards from the back of the double-sized corner lot. Not overly large, it was still the biggest house on the street, and the two-car garage made it even more impressive in a middle-class sort of way.

The magnolia leaves had lost their luster in the overcast gloom that was no longer night but not yet day. The fig and pear trees stood bare, their branches like skeletal fingers reaching upward toward the lowering clouds.

As he rounded the corner and swung down into his one-foot-on-the-pedal, other-foot-in-space coasting position, he had to alter his normal route into the driveway because of Uncle Charlie's Cadillac. It loomed up out of the semidarkness like a cargo ship out of the fog on the bay. It was awfully early for Uncle Charlie to be at the house.

He parked his bike in the garage, going quickly to the sink along the wall to run some hot water over his hands. Toweling off, he loped up the back steps through the mudroom, making sure to wipe his tennis shoes. He had a little trouble getting out of his coat because he had grown a size or two and the coat had not. Hanging it on the peg, above which was stenciled "J. B.," he stepped through the vestibule and into the large kitchen, which took up much of the back of the house. The warmth welcomed him like an old friend. And his old friend Manfred the Wonder Dog welcomed him like…well, like an old friend.

Kneeling to scratch Manfred behind the ears, he took in the tableau of a normal Saturday morning in his house. His mother was at the stove using a spatula to push some bacon grease up over the frying eggs. On the back of the stove was a pot of rice. The oven gave off the smell of biscuits almost done, and on the sideboard lay a platter with a pound or so of just-fried bacon. Off at the counter, across the room and to his right, his sister was grinding oranges on the juicer, and his brother was taking pear and fig preserves out of the refrigerator and putting them on the lazy Susan in the middle of the large table that separated him from his mother. And overlying all the smells was the odor of fresh-brewed, very strong coffee with chicory. If only he could bottle the smells of that morning, he would make a million dollars. When you're thirteen, a million dollars is about as much money as there is in the world.

"Any problems with the route?" his mother asked.

"No, ma'am. Just that dog that crazy wrestler has over on Leadyard Street. I swear he's going to get loose one day and tear my leg off."

"Well, do you want your father to go over there and speak to him?"

"No, ma'am. I guess if I can't get close enough to collect what he owes, I just won't throw him a paper, and he can ask to borrow his neighbor's or something."

His older brother PJ chimed in. "I'd call the police."

"And tell them what? I'm afraid of his dog? Can't go doing that. I bet every one of the guys with a route has at least one dog to deal with. Didn't you have a dog to mess with on your route?"

"What's that guy's name anyway?" his brother asked. "Chief Thunderstick, right?"

"No, his real name—or at least the name on the subscription—is John Tolliver. He claims to be an Apache Indian, and the name they call him in the ring is Chief Strong Wind. All I know is he has a big German shepherd, and when I go by there to collect, he sometimes threatens to sic the dog on me. So last Friday evening, when I go to collect for, like, two months he hasn't paid, you know what he says? 'I didn't subscribe to get the paper.' He tells me I've been throwing his paper for over a year and he didn't subscribe! So I show him the subscription notebook. He looks at it and tells me that's not him."

"Not him? What's that supposed to mean?" his mother asked.

"That's what I said. So he tells me his name isn't John Tolliver. It's John t-a-l-l-i-f-f-e-r-r-e-o," JB said, spelling out the Italian version of the name.

"He says his name is spelled wrong, and it's not his fault if the newspaper got it wrong. He says he doesn't owe anything, because the name is some other guy's name. And he's no more an Apache Indian than I am. His cousin is in the ninth grade over at Mae Eanes Junior High. He plays on the football team.

"I mean, I not only lose my two cents on the paper I throw him; I have to make up the thirteen cents the company gets for the paper. So every week I'm going more than a dollar in the hole just giving him a paper. Right now he owes me eight dollars and twenty cents. That's a lot of money. I'm not collecting again until next Friday, so if I don't throw him a paper, I should get his attention by then."

"Well, in a way, he's right," JB's brother said, reaching back into the refrigerator for the big bowl of butter on the bottom shelf. "You know how much you hate it when somebody around here sends us something with Jordan as our last name, or when somebody calls you Gene. It's the English inability to recognize the different sounds in our names, and so they go with the most common. There are, after all, a lot more Jordans and Genes in Mobile than there are Jourdains and Jeans."

"OK, say that's true. It still doesn't mean this guy doesn't have to pay his bill." JB stood up and, reaching for the bacon platter, broke a piece in half, took a bite, and placed the rest between his lips.

"Manfred," he mumbled, holding the bacon between his lips and bending down to the sitting dog.

Manfred reached upward with his mouth and gently took the bacon from JB's lips.

"Jean Baptiste!" His mother's raised voice was more the beginning of a laugh than a true scolding. "Stop that, or we won't have enough bacon for breakfast. Your Uncle Charlie is here."

Actually, Uncle Charlie was just his uncle by marriage. He was married to JB's father's sister, Aunt Isabelle. If Charlie had been his father's brother, he would have a French name like everyone else in the family.

JB walked over to the sink to rinse the bacon grease off. While standing there, with the warm water further restoring blood flow to his hands, he thought about his family. His real uncles were named Louis, Remy, and Etienne. They were his father's brothers. His father was Honore Baptiste, and his brother was Pierre Jouet. His sister was Margaux Emmanuelle, known to her school friends as Margie, and to her family as Me—as in the pronoun.

His mother was Francoise, and all together they were the Jourdains. A family as old as Mobile. JB's great-great-great-etc.-grandfather had been a soldier with the Sieur de Bienville and had married one of the cassette girls brought to Mobile by the French government.

Now they were all anglicized—except of course, their names. All the men were called by their initials—HB, PJ, and JB. Their mother was the only one who used her actual name. So she was Francoise to her friends, and Mrs. Honore Jourdain to strangers or casual acquaintances.

Me was home from the university for Christmas break. She was some kind of prodigy, JB explained to his friends. She was nineteen, but she had almost finished her bachelor's degree and was already taking courses for a master's. She was a whiz-bang mathematician like her father.

PJ was in his senior year at McGill High School. He was only seventeen, but he would be going to college next year, probably at Springhill, since the baseball coach there salivated every time PJ was in the room. The Dodgers had already sent an agent to talk to him about signing a contract, but PJ knew too many people who had thrown out their arms or gotten hurt or been drafted into the army to think about signing a professional contract right out of high school. He believed his future was in business, like his father.

JB was just JB. He was thirteen and in the eighth grade. His grades were good—mostly As with an occasional B sprinkled here and there. He didn't, however, show the proclivity for math his sister had, or the quick uptake and processing skills PJ evidenced. He loved to read, and he retained information like a sponge. He was always coming up with bits and pieces of trivial information about this and that. His father called him a veritable cornucopia of useless information. His mother was always telling him that he was more like her and her family—good, solid, practical, commonsense farmers. Yet she had a degree in chemistry from the university and could more than hold her own in discussions on everything from math to politics. On the latter, she was more than a little opinionated.

"Father Honore," as some of his business associates called him—mostly behind his back, because at six three and two-thirty, it wouldn't have been wise to do it to his face—was a soft-spoken individual with the patois of the port city. He almost never raised his voice, and in fact, opponents discovered that the fainter his voice became, the more trouble they were going to get. He was a fair man who insisted upon fairness all round—which made him an unlikely person to be the director of a local group of influential businessmen who managed business, politics, sports, entertainment, and other endeavors all up and down the Gulf Coast. They were in direct competition with the members of the Boston Club in New Orleans, but the Société—as it was known—was somewhat older, better organized, and in closer contact with the working-class levels of the region.

On paper, Honore owned four taxi companies (a monopoly in Mobile County), three nightclub restaurants (including the very popular Café Royale), the majority of shares in four banks, and part of the local double-A baseball team. He was as legitimate as you could be and still be successful in a world where money, name, and patronage were how you made it.

The nickname "Father" had followed him from his days at Springhill College, where it had been generally assumed that he would become either a brother or a Jesuit priest and a professor of mathematics. That he had not done so surprised more than a few of his classmates and, indeed, most of the professors at the college. Apparently, discovering women had been his downfall.

The warm water flowing over JB's hands was so soothing he would have stood there mentally climbing his family tree for several more minutes had his sister not pushed him aside with her hips while holding her hands like a doctor washing up. "Hey, squirt, move over. I need to wash this sticky juice off my hands."

He pushed back with his hips, and a battle of position began. Six years younger, he was still bigger than his sister, who, at five eight, was pretty tall for a girl. He was winning the battle until his father walked in and observed what was happening. He put his hands under JB's armpits and almost casually lifted him to the side, dropped him unceremoniously, then reached over for a table towel, which he dropped on JB's head.

"Dry your hands and leave your sister alone."

"Where's Charlie?" his wife asked.

"Gone to the Seaman's Hall for breakfast. They want him to take a ship down to Panama for somebody. Then he'll catch the next boat headed this way through the canal."

Uncle Charlie was a ship's master and sailed all over the world on cargo ships. Sometimes Aunt Isabelle went with him, but mostly she didn't. Charlie was gone sometimes for two months when he made a trip to the Orient. Lately he had been serving as a harbor pilot for Mobile Harbor, but he still took the occasional voyage as well.

"So what was so important he had to talk to you at seven o'clock on a Saturday morning?" she asked.

"What do you think?" He poured coffee from the pot into the restaurant-style cup.

"Louis?"

"Exactly. Belle wants to go with Charlie on the trip to Panama, but she's concerned about what to do with Louis. Charlie wondered if we could take him for a month or so."

"Well, I guess we could do it, although asking Dora to take on the responsibility during the day is, I think, a little too much."

"I know. Dora's a great maid, but I think she would worry too much about Louis and not get her other chores done."

"We could hire somebody," his wife mused.

"Sure we could, but without some time to get acquainted first, I'm not sure that's the best idea. Maybe I could take Louis to the office with me. Maybe that would be the best idea. He's really no trouble as long as you don't let him wander off when he's having one of his moments."

"I suppose they want to have Christmas in Panama," Francoise said.

"Yes, that's the reason Charlie was over here early. They want him to take the ship out day after tomorrow. It's an old Liberty ship like he skippered during the war, so he'll have no problems knowing the systems and such."

HB sat at the table and gently tilted the hot cup so that coffee flowed over the rim and into his saucer. He placed the cup on his plate and, taking the saucer with two hands, raised it to his lips and blew gently to cool the liquid. Then he sipped at it.

"I told him I'd pick Louis up later today." He sipped again. "You know, this whole thing could be a lot worse. What if Louis was blind or a double amputee like so many of the other guys who came home injured? What if he was bedridden and had to live in a VA home? It's been, what, fourteen years since the war? And he's done OK."

"He's done OK because you help him all the time," his wife answered. "You know it's your duty as the oldest, and I know it, and Belle knows it, but I'm not so sure about Remy or Etienne." Francoise lifted the fried eggs one at a time and slid them onto a large platter. She turned to place the platter on the table and faced HB. "I love your family dearly, but sometimes I wonder if they all depend too much on you."

It was true, JB thought. There did seem to be a lot of problems his father had to sort out for his brothers and sister. His grandparents were dead, and his father had taken over as head of the family.

His father sipped his coffee, then said, looking up over the saucer, "Well, they do some, but that's what being the oldest sibling in a family is all about—and dear, that's what I do for a living. I solve problems."

"Dad?" JB asked. "Have you heard from the navy about Uncle Louis's veteran's benefits? I thought you said they might pay him enough to hire someone to live with him full time so he didn't have to stay at Aunt Belle's."

"No, JB. We haven't heard anything other than they can't find some parts of his record. Particularly the period from when he was in the hospital at Pearl Harbor until he was evacuated from Iwo Jima."

JB's Uncle Louis had been a Marine Corps lieutenant in World War II and had come home suffering from the effects of having been wounded at Guadalcanal and then again at Iwo Jima. Something had happened to him, and he had what JB's father referred to as "spells," where he regressed into some place and time in 1943 or '44. He wasn't violent or anything; he just had conversations with people who weren't really there. Still, he could wander off looking for people or places, and since he thought he was in Hawaii or on a ship or someplace like that, he might get run over or fall or something. People didn't know how to handle it when he fell into one of the spells, and mostly they just tried to avoid him.

When he wasn't having a spell, he was—for the most part—a sad person, because he knew full well about his spells and that he couldn't hold a job. He also knew he couldn't get married or have a family, and that made him even sadder. His spells lasted from ten or fifteen minutes to three or four days. The only people who seemed to truly understand his situation were JB's father and Aunt Belle, who was Uncle Louis's fraternal twin.

JB still didn't understand how a woman could be a fraternal twin, because his Latin (he was in his third year) made it clear "fraternal" meant brother. Still, he guessed he understood that it really meant "not identical."

He sat in his chair at the table and crossed himself as his father began. "*In nomine Patris et Filii…*"

After grace, everyone passed the platters around the table or spun the lazy Susan to get the butter, jam, or preserves. There was nothing better than a fried egg on top of a big spoon of sticky rice and some crisp, thick bacon or salt pork. Biscuits with butter, pear, or homemade fig preserves, and some milk or hot coffee. It was the breakfast of champions. At least it was in the Deep South, and in December 1959 you couldn't get any further south (metaphorically) than Mobile, Alabama.

After the initial silence that falls on all tables supplied with good food, HB asked, "Did I hear somebody wouldn't pay his bill for your newspaper services?"

JB reexplained the problem with his wrestler. His father nodded and said he thought JB's plan not to throw the newspaper was a good alternative. "Let him think about it awhile. He'll come around," was all he said.

As they began to leave the table, JB asked, "Say, Dad, you don't suppose Uncle Louis is having the same problem we are, do you?"

"In what way the same problem, JB?"

"Well, I mean, maybe his records are in somebody's file whose name is Jordan or Gordon. You know how they do it. Or maybe he's got a separate file with his name spelled wrong, kind of like l-e-w-i-s for l-o-u-i-s?"

"You may have something there, JB. Although the files are supposed to be by service number, I wonder if there could be two or more files with the same service number. I've been corresponding with the Saint Louis file center so much I have a telephone number for one of the supervisors. I'll call him long distance first thing Monday and ask." He put his cup down and pushed away from the table.

"So how about you come with me to get your Uncle Louis? I know he'll be happy to see you."

"Dad, actually I see Uncle Louis almost every morning. He's always up and sitting on Aunt Belle's porch when I throw the paper. The mornings he's not there, I always think he must be having one of his spells. Otherwise, I always wave and yell out, 'Morning, Uncle Louis.' Sometimes I stop a minute to talk. He seems to like it if I do. I think he likes the early-morning smell of the bakery down the street. I always mean to go back by and offer to take him to the bakery restaurant, but I either have to get to school or, like today, the rain seemed ready to set in. But maybe we can go a little later and stop by the bakery for a doughnut and some milk."

"Sure," his father said. "We can do that. How about we go over about ten or so?"

JB went out to the garage, turned the space heater on, and began to stitch up the latest hole in one of his three newspaper bags. Then he oiled his bike and made sure he had his oilskins ready to go. He had bought a set of rain gear at the seaman's supply down near the shipyard. They would keep him dry enough, but his big problem was the papers. He pulled out the oilskin poncho he used to shelter the papers while they were in the bags on his handlebars. He would have to make sure each paper wound up on the porch in a dry spot, or he would have to get off his bike and put the paper behind the screen door for the houses that didn't have porches. It would take him much longer to throw his route tomorrow, especially since it was Sunday and the papers would be much larger. Then he went inside and began sorting out how much each subscriber owed him, and projected what he expected to collect next Friday afternoon.

By ten o'clock he had his accounts figured out and had begun to work on the paper his social studies teacher had assigned his class to have in just after New Year's: "Why War Isn't the Answer." He knew what she wanted, but he wasn't sure how to write a paper about it.

In the full light of day, the sky looked even more ominous than it had in the gloom of dawn. The clouds were low and dark gray, but it had not yet begun to rain. He suspected this would be one of those occasions where it drizzled more than it poured. He wasn't sure why, but the feeling he got was that this was more than a passing storm or front. This was a system settling in. He hoped he was wrong, but somehow he always seemed to be right about the weather. Something the sailors down at Seaman's Hall called "having a weather eye."

On the way to his aunt's house, which wasn't all that far, he asked his father, "Dad, this really isn't about money, is it? I mean, I know you have enough money to let Uncle Louis live independently, and I know you would give it to him. So why do we have to go to the trouble of trying to find his military records?"

His father thought for a moment and then pulled the car to the curb and put it in park.

"You're right, JB. It isn't about money. So if it isn't money, what do you think it's about?

"Well…" JB turned to face his father and leaned against the passenger door. "I think Uncle Louis doesn't want people to take care of him, but it isn't really about what happens now—it's about something that happened before. When I look into his eyes, it seems like his soul is wounded. Not his body and not his mind. He wants very badly to be whole, but he can't seem to make that happen. I don't think the money will make him happier, but I think it will make him feel less a burden to others. There's something else there, but what it is…?"

HB considered his son a moment and then quietly said, "JB, I think there yet may be a 'Father' in the family."

He put the car in gear, and they continued on.

In the dimness of the day, Uncle Louis seemed even sadder. He almost never smiled, even when JB made one of his excellent wordplays. It was a game JB and his father played. Puns and corny jokes. Groans were often more appreciated than actual laughs.

At the bakery shop, HB ordered six glazed doughnuts and three cups of coffee. They sat in a booth along the wall. The smell of fresh bread suffused the room as it always did. Mingled with it were undertones of fresh coffee and that wonderful aromatic scent sugared icing brings to the mix. It was a place that never failed to lift JB's spirits, yet Uncle Louis seemed determined to remain a dispirited lump. This, for JB, had become a personal challenge.

"So, Uncle Louis, why is six afraid of seven?"

"What?" his uncle asked.

"Why is six afraid of seven?" JB repeated.

"I don't know. Why is six afraid of seven?"

"Because seven ate nine." JB chuckled, his father smirked, and Uncle Louis just sat there.

Seated across from his uncle, JB was not to be denied. "And speaking of eight, is it true that you can divide it in half, square the two halves, and end up with nothing?"

His uncle looked quizzical but only for a moment.

"If you mean you take the zero top half of the figure eight and the zero bottom half and square either or both to arrive at a final answer of zero, then the answer is yes."

"Oh, you've heard it." JB deadpanned, then looked sideways at his father. "Dad, are you stealing my jokes again?"

"Steal them? Why on earth would I steal them? I have plenty of my own bad jokes!"

The interplay drew the briefest and slightest of grins from Louis.

"Aha!" JB shouted and pointed at his uncle. "I saw it. He grinned." Leaning over and looking earnestly in his uncle's eyes, he continued. "Now see here, Uncle Louis. If you're going to spend Christmas with us, we don't allow anybody to feel sad over Christmas. It's a rule in the house that even if you don't feel happy, you have to pretend. Right, Dad?"

His father looked a little taken aback by JB's forthrightness but quickly recovered and supported his son. "Absolutely, house rules. Everybody acts happy during Christmas."

"So, Uncle Looouis"—JB dragged the name out a full second—"I'm going to loan you a joke book, and every day you're going to tell at least two, count 'em, two jokes while we're in a family situation. Right, Dad?'

"Oh yes, absolutely. Two, no less!" His father was getting into the spirit.

"Yes, two jokes. You will have practiced them so that your delivery is good, and you will not read them. Two jokes a day. You must obtain a laugh or at least a decent groan. If you need help, I'll be there. I suggest you not ask your older brother, because he can't tell a joke without sniggling before he gets to the punch line."

"What do you mean, sniggling? Why, I'll have you know I have them rolling on the floor in the office."

"Wouldn't have a thing to do with you being the boss, would it?"

The bantering continued, and it seemed that what made Louis smile the most wasn't the jokes, good or bad, but the spirited battle between father and youngest son, each striving to topple the other from his perceived acme of humor. And realizing this, father and son played it to the hilt so that by the time they returned home, Louis, while not Mr. Enthusiasm, wasn't Mr. Let-Me-Wallow-in-My-Depression either.

Dinner and an evening in front of the fireplace, with HB telling stories about Louis as a child, helped them bond as a family settling in to celebrate Christmas.

The next morning the mist started a little after three. By four thirty it had developed into a steady drizzle and, as JB had prophesied, looked as if it was there to stay awhile. It was wet, and it was cold. This, unfortunately, was winter in Mobile. Forty degrees and 100 percent humidity—or as close to that as you can get when it's raining. The night air was so heavy with moisture JB almost felt resistance as he pedaled out of the garage.

The boys rolled into the substation pretty much on time. Somebody had lit a fire in an old fifty-gallon drum, and while they'd have liked to stand by the drum to get warm, it was just outside the overhang, and to get near, they had to stand in the drizzle. Those with appropriate rain gear didn't mind. They stood close by the drum, letting the drizzle trickle down their oilskin helmets and into the mud, which had been stirred to a gummy consistency by their rubber deck boots. Those with skimpier rain hats and coats, or with no rubber boots, would turn their collars up, hunch in the rain for a few moments near the drum, and then scamper back to the open-sided shelter.

The distributor finally arrived in the delivery truck and began tossing the bundles of papers onto the concrete floor of the shelter. JB had to find his bundles—those that said "Route SE-5"—cut the wires that held the bundles together, and then fold each paper. But since these were Sunday papers, he had to roll each one, put a rubber band around the paper, and then stand it upright in his delivery bag. He had to buy the rubber bands, so he guessed that on Sundays he made less than two cents a paper—but you couldn't lease a route just for Monday through Saturday.

Once he had all the papers rolled up and stowed, he had filled two bags and part of the third. He placed the first bag on the front of his bike, the strap up and over his upturned handlebars. He set the second bag securely into the top of the first and hung the strap of the third around his neck, with the bag resting on the crossbar of his bike. He put the poncho over the two bags on his handlebars, with the tail tucked in over the third bag and against his chest. The head flap on the poncho was over the second bag, allowing access to the papers while still protecting them from most of the rain.

He pushed off, standing to pedal to get the heavy load under way, then settled back onto his seat, keeping a steady pace for the two miles he had to cover to reach his route. The rain stung his face, but that didn't last long, because the cold was making it numb. By the time he had gone a mile, his nose had begun to run, and he wiped at it with the left sleeve of his raincoat.

He reached the entry point to his route and began to carefully wind his way in and out of the driveways and sidewalks, ensuring every throw made cover. The last thing he wanted was to have to stop, try to steady his bike in an upright position, and recover a misthrown paper. He thought about just throwing another paper from his bag since he usually had about six extras and didn't think he would make that many errors. Still, he would lose money if he did, and he wasn't about losing money.

One nice thing about a cold rain was the dogs were under cover and didn't like coming out any more than JB liked being out. Toward the end of his route, he passed Aunt Belle's house, which looked dark since Uncle Louis wasn't on the porch waiting for the paper. He'd have to remember not to throw them a paper while they were gone to Panama.

When he was done, he knew every paper—all hundred and fifty of them—had reached a covered spot, even though he had almost turned the bike over three or four times while straddling the crossbar as he stopped and reached to open a screen door to place the paper. Still, he knew somebody would call the paper and tell them he or she had received a wet paper that morning. He would find out about it at the brief meeting on Monday morning at the substation.

As he exited his route, he could smell the bakery. In the drizzle the aroma was even sweeter than usual, and the air just a little warmer. Nothing would have pleased him more than to slide into a booth and order some hot doughnuts and coffee, but he was on his way to Saint Matthews for the eight o'clock Mass. He was the acolyte for Father Sheen, so he needed to get there, change out of his rain gear and into a cassock and cotta, and then check to ensure the cruets, the lavabo, the towels, and all the other things associated with Communion had been placed correctly by the altar guild. They always were, but it was his job to check.

There were few people at the eight o'clock Mass because of the rain. Ordinarily there would have been forty or fifty people wanting to get their required Mass done and get on to other Sunday chores, but this morning there were barely twenty.

Done with the Mass, he pedaled home. The rain was heavier but still not a downpour. It smacked his oilskin helmet enough to sound like woodpeckers working on a dead tree, and it was still very cold. Taking off his rain gear in the garage, he made sure the space heater was on so that his gear would dry and be warm when he had to put it on again. He knew the rain was here for a while and anticipated that at least Monday and Tuesday would be wet throws.

The house was empty save for Manfred the Wonder Dog, who greeted him as a hero returned from a long absence. His mother had left a covered plate on the sideboard with some cold bacon and biscuits. He turned the gas on under the coffeepot and waited for it to warm. Meanwhile, he stuffed some bacon in a biscuit and grabbed some pear preserves out of the refrigerator. When the coffee was hot, he poured a cup and sat down to read the paper he had brought in with him. Manfred sat with his head on JB's knee, accepting the occasional bite of bacon as rings from the king to a thane.

Finishing the paper (there was little of interest), JB decided to try to work on his school assignment. He sat at his desk, sharpening his pencil, arranging his notebook, and writing the assignment topic on the front of the notebook. He did everything but start on the assignment. He got no further than he had gotten previously. He thought he knew what the teacher wanted, but he wasn't sure how to write it.

At one, his parents were home, and there was work to be done in the kitchen for Sunday dinner. Today they were having red snapper, rice, sweet-and-sour onion relish, winter squash, some fresh rolls from the bakery, and for dessert, blackberry-and-apple pie with some of the blackberries his mom had put up this summer.

After dinner they adjourned to the living room, where Me played the piano. She was as good on the piano as she was at extrapolating logarithms. The room was large, but the smell of the Christmas tree was everywhere. The fireplace was across the room from the piano, and they all sat with their backs to the music and their faces to the fire. HB went over to the piano and began to sing as Me played. He had a wonderful baritone voice, and his accent was perfect for the music. He sang "Ave Maria" beautifully.

JB had more appreciation for the music than would the typical thirteen-year-old. He struggled every Wednesday afternoon to master the keys but never hoped to be as good as Me or HB. Something about math skills and music. His mother had a lovely voice but seldom sang unless she was in a group. PJ played the guitar as well as the piano, but he too was not in the same class as his father and sister.

After the song, HB went upstairs and came down with a small but long case. He set it on the piano and opened it. It was a King silver clarinet. He played clarinet himself, but once he put the bell on this instrument, he took a new reed from a packet, put it on the mouthpiece, and handed the clarinet to Louis, who at first refused it but, after the right entreaties from everyone, took it and stuck the mouthpiece in his mouth to wet the reed. After a minute or so, he blew a major scale, then a chromatic one. HB sat down at the piano and played the first four bars of "Stardust." He looked at Louis and started again, and this time a full-toned, throaty clarinet captured the melody and sent it wafting into the ether of time, warping the continuum—and it was 1938.

Louis watched his brother as he played. He did not close his eyes to remember the tune but seemed rather to watch the music from the bell of his metal clarinet as it floated toward the ceiling and into the invisible beyond. When he held the last note before sending it off to follow the others, there was a tear in his eye. That was quickly dried, though, and followed by sweat when HB launched into "St. James Infirmary" and Louis was doing runs up and down the keys. Louis was skilled and, even if out of practice, a remarkable clarinet player. At the end he was out of breath but seemed livelier than JB could remember seeing him in…well, forever. He was like a really cool person.

⚜

On Monday morning, JB once again had a wet throw. Not much different from Sunday, but the papers were smaller. They occupied only a bag and a half.

Monday afternoon JB went Christmas shopping, hitting all the stores in downtown Mobile. He used an umbrella instead of his rain helmet, but he wore his deck boots because Mobile floods with only a minimal amount of rain, and while this was only a drizzle, there were still fairly deep places along the curbs and intersections where his normal loafers or tennis shoes would have become waterlogged. He kept the rain helmet in the bag he carried because he had to wear it when traveling to and from home. You couldn't carry an opened umbrella on a bike unless you were one of those guys in the circus riding a unicycle.

A scarf for his mother, some sheet music for Me, and a box of picks for PJ. He already had a gift for his father. It was a tin box with a picture of their house painted on it. JB had traded one of his customers three months' worth of free newspapers to do it. It was a great gift, and one he knew his father would value.

One gift from each—that was the rule in the Jourdain family. Christmas wasn't some sort of extravaganza with piles of gifts under the tree beforehand and jungles of wrapping paper and ribbon afterward. Santa Claus was more like the Holy Ghost. He was the bringer of the spirit of Christmas, which was love and brotherhood. Early on, the Jourdain children learned it was more appropriate to ask Santa Claus to take care of the less fortunate, and every year they selected a group they would ask Santa to help. Then, like magic, on Christmas morning they would find a note from Santa on the tree telling them how he had arranged for the children at the Catholic orphanage to have toys this Christmas, or that he had helped the children at Saint Joseph's Hospital, or that food had been sent to the group of families the children had selected. It was a fine way to celebrate Christmas, and there was no reason to ever stop believing in Santa, since he worked like the Holy Ghost.

Now JB had to come up with a gift for his uncle. Nothing he had seen in any of the stores caught his eye. On his way home, his other gifts secured against the rain under his oilskin poncho, he passed an antiques shop on Conti Street. Well, the sign said "Antiques," but to JB it looked more like a junk shop than an antiques shop. It did have an awning under which he could rest his bike, so he went in. An antiques shop in a port city is not unlike an exotic pawnshop. Sailors bring in all manner of items, wanting to sell them to the owner. JB browsed through the store, occasionally asking the price on this or that item. There were no other customers, so he had the full attention of the shop's owner.

"Do you know what you're looking for?"

"Not really, I'm just browsing. I need a Christmas gift for my uncle."

"Do you have a price in mind?"

"Not really. I mean, not a piece of furniture or anything like that."

"Would you like to look at something like a dagger from the Middle East?"

"Not really. He doesn't need a dagger."

"Do you know what he needs?"

"Not really. That's why I'm browsing."

The owner mentally threw up his hands and left JB to wander the extremely tight aisles of the store.

As he turned from one aisle into another, JB came face-to-face with a statute of Vishnu. He recognized it from a book his father had in his library entitled *Hinduism, the Catholic Faith of the East*. The statue momentarily transfixed him. His mental apparatus jumped ahead, and JB was suddenly remembering a book he liked yet didn't like. A book that had more impact on his thought than even Dostoevsky's *Crime and Punishment*. The book was *The Razor's Edge*, by W. Somerset Maugham. JB was upset with himself that he hadn't seen the parallels between not just Larry Darrell but also Gray and Sophie and his Uncle Louis before. Still, he did not think his uncle was experiencing a crisis of finding meaning in life. It was something else, something that amalgamated all three character crises but displayed different symptoms.

Then JB knew what he wanted to get Uncle Louis.

"Have you got any old coins from India? Rather large ones, I think."

⚜

Friday, the weather continued to emulate a New England fall. It remained in the forties, and the humidity made it seem even colder. JB, wrapped up in his too-small coat, made his collection rounds. It was two days till Christmas, and nobody wanted to part with money, especially his subscribers who lived in the Byrd Housing Project, but grumbling, they paid their bills. As he was pedaling down Leadyard Street, the wrestler ran out of his house.

"Kid! Hey, kid! Stop!"

JB pulled up, putting his right foot on the curb. The wrestler came outside his chain link fence. In his hand he held several dollar bills.

"Hey, kid, I need to pay my bill, but I forgot what I owe ya."

JB, somewhat surprised, pulled his account book from his coat pocket. "Eight dollars and twenty cents," he said.

"Oh, only eight dollars?" the wrestler said.

"And twenty cents," JB added.

"Well, look, here's eight fifty. You can keep the change."

JB reached down to his belt and punched out a quarter and a nickel from his belt coin changer.

"I'm sorry, sir, but we're not allowed to accept gratuities," he said, handing the change to the man.

"Oh, right. Well, listen, kid, there's a couple more things. I mean, you know I'm only having you on about the dog. I would never let him hurt you. I mean, he's really a good family dog. Just a little too protective. And, oh yeah, the last thing. You'll see that my subscription gets entered in the right name, you know, t-a-l-l-i-f-f-e-r-r-e-o. I wouldn't want there to be any misunderstanding."

He turned to go back into his house.

JB pushed away from the curb, encouraged that his plan had worked so well.

As he pedaled away from the house, an enormous dark-blue Lincoln pulled out of a side street and headed back to town. The rather large man at the wheel was grinning from ear to ear. HB had been right: the wrestler wasn't actually such a tough guy, at least not when a really tough guy asked him nicely to do something.

⚜

The day before Christmas Eve, HB gathered the family in the living room after dinner. If "the cat who swallowed the canary" described someone pleased with himself, then this cat had feasted on an entire aviary.

"The supervisor I spoke with on Monday called me back today. Louis, they found your records. Apparently they were filed under 'Lewis Jordan,' just as JB suggested. Seems you are in for some back pay and a couple of medals. Well, actually not just any old medals: two Silver Stars for gallantry. You were promoted to captain while you were on Iwo Jima, and you should have been medically retired, not just discharged with a disability. The supervisor showed the errors to *his* supervisor, and they're going to suggest the secretary of the navy present you the medals. He read me the recommendations for the medals, and Louis, you're a real hero. I mean, really a hero. Why haven't you told us about this?"

HB was too excited to notice the look in Louis's eyes, but JB caught it as Louis tried very hard to smile. It wasn't the look of a man relieved. It was more like a man trapped in a corner of an alley with nowhere to run. A little sliver of understanding revealed itself to JB.

By Christmas Eve the rain had stopped, but the wind had increased, and the clouds still hugged the ground like a wife seeing her husband off to war. The family would gather for an early-afternoon meal and then again to go to midnight Mass at the basilica. In between was the final wrapping of gifts, and JB would make sure he took a nap. He didn't want to miss any of what would follow. After Mass they would go to Café Royale. In years past, a small staff of volunteers would have cooked up a breakfast feast for the family. Now it was just cafés au lait and fresh beignets and maybe some scrambled eggs with crawfish and onions. For JB they always had a pot of hominy grits and lots of fresh butter. There was banana pudding, and he who found the piece of hard candy in his pudding would be awarded the first gift on Christmas morning. Thus fortified, the family would return home to eventually find their way to bed.

⚜

Theirs was not the "up at the crack of dawn" Christmas celebration of other homes but one of "up by ten o'clock" for coffee and croissants. Then everyone dressed, and by eleven thirty or so, they were in the living room to open stockings and gifts.

The rain had returned during the early-morning hours. Once again it was a cold drizzle that made people glad of being inside, especially if they had a fireplace. HB handed Me the first gift. It was JB's sheet music. Me insisted on kissing JB, which he had only recently found the fortitude not to resist. JB's scarf to his mom was the second gift, and he had to endure another kiss. Thus it went until JB was handed a gift longer and wider than it was high. Removing the gift wrap revealed only a box like the kind shirts come in, but larger. Taking the top off, he found a genuine US Army Air Forces A-2 bomber jacket. When he put it on, it was just a little too large.

"So you can wear it longer," his mother said.

"Did you notice the nameplate?" his father asked.

JB looked down, and sewn on the left side of the breast was an actual leather nameplate. It read, in gold letters, "J. B. Jourdain." JB beamed. He couldn't think of a better Christmas present. Well, maybe one, but that wasn't his father's or mother's to give.

The very next gift was JB's for his father, and there was a misting of eyes when the box was passed around. No kiss from his father but a bear hug that engulfed him and during which he could have sworn he heard a slight sigh.

The small box for Louis from JB was presented next.

"Uncle Louis, don't open that right now," JB said. "A little later, maybe after dinner."

Everyone adjourned to the kitchen to help with Christmas dinner. Marlin steaks with béarnaise sauce, steamed onions and apples, cheese grits made with aged Gouda, marinated artichoke hearts, and for dessert, pear tarts with sweet whiskey sauce. Everyone but JB drank a fine French Chardonnay. JB had a glass of pear cider that he found overly tart but declined to criticize.

Then, after dinner, everyone gathered once again in the living room, where HB passed around his famous planter's punch, which even JB was allowed to sample.

The rain became heavier, and with the wind, it attacked the windowpanes. A shutter came loose, and JB and PJ ran to the front porch to secure it. Other shutters bumped and banged as the wind tore at their moorings. It had become a stormy night.

Late in the evening, when everyone had gone off to do something else, JB asked his uncle to open the gift. The small box revealed the coin. It was a large—as in silver dollar–sized—bronze coin from the reign of the Mughal ruler Akbar the Great. JB had bartered hard for the coin with the owner of the store, finally wearing him down with the story of how he wished to use the coin. At that, the owner had taken a chance and told JB he would sell him the coin for whatever money JB had in his pocket. Having already purchased his other Christmas gifts, JB had six dollars remaining in his pocket, and he thought that an excellent bargain. He didn't know how the shop owner felt. Still, there it was.

Uncle Louis took it from the box. It shone brightly in the light from the fireplace. JB, knowing that he was destroying the patina of age, had boiled the coin in hot salt water and then scrubbed it clean and polished it with Brasso so now it looked as if it had just been stamped by hammer and mold. He cared not about patina but rather about shine.

"That coin is magical," JB said.

"Really? Magical?" Uncle Louis held the coin between his thumb and forefinger and looked at it in the light of the fireplace. "Magical, you say. How so? And remember, JB, I read *The Razor's Edge*. In fact, didn't you see me reading it one morning and ask me about it?"

"Oh sure, I remember, but this coin isn't like the coin in that story. Only the character Gray thought that coin was magical. Everybody else knew it was just a coin. But this coin has honest-to-goodness magical properties. Of course, the magic only works if you believe in it. Do you believe in magic, Uncle Louis?"

"I don't think so, Jean." Louis used JB's given name, and JB could tell Louis was drifting toward one of his spells. JB had to keep him in the present.

"But you do believe in God. I saw you at Mass last night. You're angry with him, but you still believe in him. Well, maybe magic is very small miracles, and God makes miracles possible. It's too complicated for me to explain, but I just know it. It's as real as anything else if you know where to look."

JB was on his knees between the sofa and the fireplace. Louis sat on the front edge of the sofa. JB leaned forward and took the coin. He held it so the light from the fireplace was reflected off the shiny bronze of the coin and onto the ceiling.

"Think about it, Uncle Louis. Someone held this coin in front of a fire five hundred years ago. Perhaps it cast its light onto a tent or maybe onto the ceiling in Akbar's palace. How did he come by the coin? Did he steal it? Beg it? Borrow it? Earn it? Did he sell his goods or produce for it? Was it a tax? Who was that man? What problems did he have? How did he die? What was his legacy? Was he brigand or prince? Farmer or merchant? Beggar or holy man? Perhaps this coin has been held in the hand of all of those and more. Think about it."

JB turned the coin slightly so that the reflection traveled along the ceiling and down onto the wall.

"This coin enables time travel. It takes our minds back five hundred years or four hundred years or two hundred years, and we find ourselves in bazaars or palaces or maybe in the tent of a desert brigand. We seek to know, our mind's eye inquiring. Our imaginations are fueled by the extrapolation of our knowledge. We are there. But to come home, we simply put the coin away." JB dropped the coin into his sweater pocket, and the reflection stopped traveling down the wall.

"It's that simple, Uncle Louis. It's great to go into the past, but we have to have a way home. This coin does that."

Louis, a wistful, almost-enigmatic smile on his face, took JB's hand. "I know you think you understand, but I don't think it's quite that simple. I wish it were."

"Oh, but it is," JB countered. "Dad told me about the recommendations for the Silver Stars. It seems that in both cases, lots of people you liked or knew died, even though you tried to save them. The citation says that you were cut off behind enemy lines and suffered from cerebral malaria. That you were wounded by shellfire but continued to lead your troops. You were wounded again on Iwo Jima and suffered a relapse of the malaria after stopping a Japanese counterattack.

"Uncle Louis, I'm only thirteen, and I wish I understood better, but I know it doesn't do any good being mad at God. Besides, I don't think it's God you're mad at. Like Larry and Sophia in *The Razor's Edge*, you think it's wrong that somebody else died and you didn't. On the one hand you feel guilty, on the other you feel cheated—but neither is right.

"There may not be anything you can do about the relapse spells, but I think that if you want to come back sooner, you can. Just keep the coin in your pocket, and know that you can come back anytime you choose."

JB stood up, leaned over, and hugged his uncle, then headed upstairs to his bedroom.

HB, who had been listening at the French doors into the dining room, entered quietly and sat next to his younger brother. Louis had tears in his eyes. HB put his arm around him and pulled him over so that Louis's head was on his shoulder.

⚜

Upstairs JB sat at his desk. He took his notebook out and began to write:

Why War Isn't the Answer

> A twenty-year-old left his home in the beautiful port city of Mobile to defend his country in a war the country didn't want and tried to avoid. A twenty-year-old with exceptional musical talent, with the potential of youth, and with the future in his eyes…

# Fairies in the Garden

⚜

He put down the pen, and while he waited for the ink to dry, he looked out the window at the garden. Bare now, it would begin coming back to life in a couple of weeks. Already the green shoots of the jonquils, crocuses, and tulips were a couple of inches out of the ground. A warm spell was forecast for the end of the month, so he knew there would be a literal explosion of color in the beds. He looked forward to it. While winter had not been particularly bad this year, he always looked forward to the vibrant colors of spring—almost as much as he welcomed the masculine colors of fall. That's how he saw the seasons. Spring was feminine, fall was masculine, and summer was neuter. Winter—well, winter was that fourth category of gender that some languages have. It was just winter.

He took up his field glasses and looked at the clumps of maiden grass on the hill behind the garden. There should be one or two sprigs of green grass beginning to make their way through the two-foot stubble that had been left after the grasses were cut in the winter. He didn't see any yet, but then, that didn't mean they weren't there. There might be some on the uphill side of the grasses—the side he couldn't see from his chair. He didn't worry, for the grasses were the most dependable of the plants he had put in ten years ago. The other perennials were dependable as well, and by midspring, the house would be full of bouquets of cut flowers. He had great hopes for his roses this year. He was also going to try some baby's breath so that his bouquets would have a more finished look to them.

In his mind, he could already see the bouquets arranged in the crystal vases he and his wife had accumulated over the past quarter century. He always gave her something crystal for Christmas, and many years that something had been a new vase. She enjoyed the garden, and he allowed her to think it was hers. Thus the small poem he had recently crafted and had just written inside the card he would give her for Easter. Looking at the card under glancing light, he put it back on his desk and proofread it:

### *A Garden Rock*

> I put it here, I put it there,
> I put it almost everywhere.
> "No, no!" she says. "I think…"
> And then, before I blink,
> She has me lift it yet again,
> And now I put it near the drain.
> "It's a rock," I tell her, tuckered out.
> "No, no!" she cries. "Not near the spout!"

Yesterday, it was a bench.
And now she wants it near the fence.
Quasimodo-like, I lift once more—
My eyes glance toward the kitchen door—
"A rock!" I cry. "It is a rock, my dearest."
"Yes, yes!" She smiles. "A most unusual rock.
It must be prominent so all who regard
Will see my garden is not just a yard."

I lift again, but in pain I drop
The rock upon my toes. "Stop!
Stop!" she cries. "For that's the place!"
She regards it as if it shines in grace.
She looks at it from here, she considers it from there,
She looks from almost everywhere.
In anticipation of relief, I lean upon the fence—
Then hear with dread—"But now, about that bench…"

Yes, the bench had gone here, and there, much like the rock—well, rocks, actually. There were rocks as accent points in many parts of the segregated garden: some large, some small, but all perfectly placed to accentuate the flow of the pea-gravel paths and raised beds. And now there were several benches as well; each garden section possessed its own seating areas. Benches, varnished cut-tree-trunk portions, even a rock or two—all suitable for sitting. He had not, of course, moved those. They had been jobs for a forklift. It was, indeed, not just a yard.

The fruit trees had grown sufficiently so that one could now seat oneself under them for shade on a hot summer day. But in the summer, when the fruit was ripe, the bees could be off-putting. Then he would sit under one of the larger trees on the periphery of the garden. A pecan tree and a white oak gave nice shade, and these were on the hill, so the entire garden was displayed below them. Still, getting up the hill could be a problem. He so much wanted to be able to do for himself, but even with two canes it was difficult. Then, coming down, he often felt as if he might tumble headfirst as the rocks slipped beneath the rubber tips of his canes. Most times, his disease was just a nuisance, but sometimes—just sometimes—it made him angry, and his anger would give way to frustration, and frustration to tears.

It was just self-pity, he told himself, and he had never been one for self-pity. But when the emotion overwhelmed him, it was difficult to fight it off. Today, though, there was hope for the spring—and he swung himself around deftly, just missing the small table with the vase of dried pink dogwood and forsythia blooms. He hobbled off to find the stack of plant catalogs that had come in the mail. He wanted some different butterfly flowers this year, and if one didn't order early, one didn't get them. En route, he passed his favorite chair—to which he promised a quick return once he had gathered the catalogs.

His wife woke him with a kiss on his forehead. Some of the catalogs remained in his lap; others had slipped to the floor. She stooped to pick them up.

"Beautiful flowers!" She held up the cover of a catalog that displayed a picture of a street floral boutique with racks of colorful bouquets sticking out of white wrapping paper. A purple banner hanging from the boutique tent announced "FLOWERS"—and there were, indeed, flowers everywhere.

"This," she said, "reminds me of your stories about the French Market when you were young."

He looked hard at the picture. Squinting, he closed down his peripheral vision so that the picture became his only field of focus. Yes, it did look a little as some of the stalls at the French Market in New Orleans had looked when he was twelve.

"Yes, you're right. It does look like the Market. It was just two blocks from my Aunt Louise's house on Chartres Street. In those days, it was just a covered concrete slab with a lot of stalls, and the farmers used to bring their produce in, to sell it to the people of the city. There were people selling all sorts of things, but mostly it was fruits, and vegetables, and flowers—lots of flowers."

His wife moved to the fireplace and turned on the gas fire, then to the bar, where she poured out two portions of single malt—one for him and one for herself. Then she sat in her chair, for she knew he would now tell the story again, and she would listen. She loved to hear him talk. He would tell the story, and the sun would set—leaving them in a darkened world, the night held at bay only by the light of the fire and the warmth of his accent.

"My daddy used to send me from our home in Mobile over to New Orleans, to help my Aunt Louise." He began, then stopped to smell, then sample the Balvenie she had poured. "Aunt Louise was a widow. Her husband—now mind you I didn't know her husband, because he was killed in the war. Well, anyway, her husband had been a first mate in the merchant marine for quite some time, and then the war happened, and they started building Liberty ships. And those ships needed captains, so he became a captain of a Liberty cargo ship and made several convoy runs to Russia and England. He would go off for months at a time, but he always came home to the small house they had on Chartres Street in the French Quarter. Of course, the Quarter wasn't quite the year-round tourist trap then that it is now. Some of the Quarter could be rough. Mardi Gras was always a big time in the Quarter, but the rest of the year it was just the Quarter. Food and booze, gambling and prostitution, jazz and Dixieland. Those were the businesses you found in the Quarter.

"So Aunt Louise is a widow, and she's got this small house on Chartres Street—but I've said that already. Well, it's not much, but it's two-story brick and has a brick wall separating it from the street. Up on the second-story landing, it has some decent ironwork railings and such. It's not a bad house, as houses in the Quarter go. Now, my father had tried to move Aunt Louise back home to Mobile, but she wouldn't come. She insisted that Captain Delacroix—that was her husband's name, Remy Delacroix—would still come home, and if she moved back to Mobile, he wouldn't be able to find her.

"Now, Aunt Louise was as sharp as a tack in most things, but in this one particular area, there was just no reasoning with her. She was adamant that the captain would come home, even though the war had been over for fourteen years. She kept a freshly pressed uniform in the closet of the master bedroom with a polished set of dress shoes and a shirt that got washed and ironed once a week and changed out when its cuffs and collar began to fray from those washings. When she bought groceries, it was always enough for two, just in case he was to arrive unannounced. Other than that, she was pretty normal—except, that is, for talking to the fairies in the garden. She could sit for hours on a bench in her small garden and converse with this fairy or that. But I'm getting ahead of myself.

"I didn't know a lot of this until I was twelve and my father asked if I thought I was big enough to go over to New Orleans and help Aunt Louise with her garden and some other things that might need doing. Well, of course I said right away that I was, indeed, big enough. So my father took me down to the bus station and bought a ticket on the Greyhound bus. 'Now don't you get off in Pascagoula or Biloxi,' he said. 'Make sure you're in New Orleans, and make sure your aunt is there to meet you.'

"Of course, I asked him how I was supposed to ensure my aunt was there to meet me. 'Don't be precocious,' he said. Now, how was I to be precocious when I didn't yet know the meaning of the word? Still, I reckoned that what he meant was not to leave the bus station until Aunt Louise arrived, and I assured him that I would not.

"Well, it wasn't a worry anyway, because she was there, and we took the trolley buses back to the Quarter. There's a famous trolley—well, it's famous now anyway, because of Tennessee Williams's play *A Streetcar Named Desire*. We rode on the Desire Route, but we rode on a bus, not a streetcar.

"So before I left, my father told me about my aunt and Captain Delacroix. He told me that my aunt had become 'pixilated' because the fairies had not wanted her to suffer from the grief of the loss of her husband. That's why my dad didn't insist that my aunt move to Mobile. He was afraid the fairies might not come, and then my aunt would grieve until she, too, died. At first, I laughed when my father told me about the fairies, but when I saw the look on his face, I understood he was serious. 'How can a grown man believe in fairies?' I asked myself. Not just a grown man, but my father!

"So I already knew about the fairies when Aunt Louise told me the next morning. We were in the garden, and she was asking me to do some weeding and some thinning—showing me which plants to pull as weeds and which to thin. We were also deadheading coneflowers and mums and such. Then she wanted me to rake the pea gravel and to take out all the leaves and other kinds of trash that end up in those small rock walkways. You know—we have the people who help us now do it every day. Anyway, I was to be careful of the toad houses and certain plants and small water features along the paths. I was to clean and put fresh water into those small containers, but I was also to be quiet and attentive so as not to disturb the fairies there.

"I did as I was told. There was no heavy work, and had it not been summer and New Orleans, I doubt I would have worked up much of a sweat. But it was summer, so I did work up a sweat, and I thought that perhaps if I rose earlier, then I could have the tasks done before the sun became hot. Plus, I would have more time for myself, to explore. Aunt Louise encouraged me to see the city, the river, the Quarter, and all the sights. At night, I could hear the jazz from a place on the next corner over, and it encouraged me to move about.

"The house was hot and humid at night, cooling only in the early-morning hours. Once I had cleaned the garden and the shed, there was not much in the way of work—except to run the occasional shopping errand for Aunt Louise. Thus, one morning, after having moved a few fallen leaves from the walkways and swept the front porch, I wandered down to the French Market. The sun had just come up, and the farmers were still unloading their produce. I offered to help and, after lifting a few boxes, earned a dollar. The next morning, I got there earlier and earned a dollar more. The third morning, I rose before the sun—when the damp was still cool—and went to the Market. There was a man hosing down the stalls, and I asked if he needed help. That morning I made four dollars. By the time the sun was clearing the Mississippi Bridge the following mornings, I was actually ending my work and was on my way to the Café Du Monde.

"Now the Café Du Monde, in those days, was a small coffee shop, but it was already famous for its sugared beignets, which, of course, you could get elsewhere in the city. But Café Du Monde is right by the Cathedral, so it got a lot of business. When I was in New Orleans, the waitresses at the café were mostly Acadian and Creole, so they tended to speak with thick accents—and they all spoke the local French well. So, big man that I was at twelve, and with cash needing to be spent, I'd stroll in and announce to one and all of the waitresses, '*Trois beignets et café au lait, ma cherie.*' While I ate the beignets, I learned to flirt, since the waitresses were always flirting with me. I learned to speak Acadian French well enough, and I learned what was happening in the real New Orleans, not the tourist version of the city. I always left a fifteen-cent tip. Now, that was big spending!

"In the evenings, it was back to help load up and clean the stalls again. Four more dollars but also, more importantly, lots of leftover flowers, from which I would make two or three nice bouquets, which I took to Aunt Louise's house and placed in vases and, when I ran out of vases, in mason fruit jars. The house was always perfumed and colorful. I've liked cut-flower bouquets ever since.

"After supper, we would sit out in the garden for a while. Just my aunt and me. I listened to her talk to the fairies, and once or twice, my eyes caught the movement of what might have been tiny wings—but I assured myself that it was just my imagination, and nothing more. One evening my aunt retired early, and I sat alone in the garden, not yet wanting to climb into a bed that would quickly become all too hot. The bench wasn't all that comfortable, but that night it seemed like a nice club chair. I caught myself once or twice dozing off and then finally woke and decided I would go to bed. But there was something I couldn't quite get out of my head—something that was either a dream or perhaps a half remembrance of something my aunt had said. There were fairies, and in my dream I had seen them cavorting through the garden, inviting me to join them.

"The next day I told my aunt about the dream, and she was quick to explain that fairies first found their way into our world through our dreams. She seemed most rational when she said it. So rational that it sounded almost logical to me. So for many evenings after, I sat in her garden inviting fairies to attend me—but I never had the same experience again. When I finally left New Orleans in late August, my aunt gave me a toad house and a cutting of a plant in her garden that she said was a favorite of the fairies. I promised her I would put it in our garden at home, and I did. And, my dear, as you know, there has always been a descendant of that plant in our own garden, grown from a cutting from in my father's garden."

He sat back in his chair, the story told once more. His legs hurt; it was time for his evening medication. He finished the Balvenie and rose with the difficulty of a cripple. The arms of the large leather chair acted as bases for his still-strong shoulders. But he knew it was only a matter of time before his arms, too, would begin to fail him.

After dinner, he returned to his desk to envelope the Easter card. While it was still only the beginning of Lent, he felt he needed to finish some tasks he had set himself—and cards with poems were a tradition he had established with his wife more than thirty years ago. She had boxes of his sophomoric verse stashed in her closet.

After he had sealed her card in its envelope, he searched briefly and, finding the book he sought, took out the sheet of paper on which his precocious fifteen-year-old hand had written long ago:

### *I Know They're Here*

A white gardenia left upon my sill,
A gossamer wing discarded,
Tiny movements caught when I sit very still,
A sense of time and place well guarded.

A ring below the oaks around,
Dew on a web so finely spun,
Murmurings heard near the ground.
Perhaps I am a chosen one!

To see and to converse a bit
Would make me a contented man.
I have time now, a while to sit
And seek their wisdom if I can.

I know they're here.
My father said as much
When whispering in my ear
Of Mab, Titania, Oberon, and such.

I know it's Puck I hear
When tight I close my eyes and listen.

His laughter's almost crystal clear
As he dares me nab him, eyes a-glisten.

Many times has wee Mab shown her face
As I nodded on the bench.
My dreams in many colors have raced.
Not yet, though, have I crossed the fence.

Yet my faith is I'll find the stile
That will take me to their land.
It's near, I think, and in a while
Oberon will sit himself at hand.

Puck will gambol, twirl, and dance.
Bess will sing, her tiny voice ringing.
I'll look on, as if from a trance,
And quick I'll find my troubles fleeing.

But I must not stay too long,
For fey I would not become.
Still, should I find them in their song,
I must remain until they're done.

Turning off his desk lamp, he stared into the moon and the starlit garden. He considered the verse again, not needing to read, for he had memorized it long ago. He smiled at the thought that at fifteen he had actually known what "gambol" meant and that the New Orleans and Mobile public libraries had had, if not extensive, at least adequate collections of books on faeries, fairies, elves, and pixies.

Once again, his focus closed down, and now just the silver-gray, moonlit bench in the middle of the garden existed. For fey he would not become. He had written of it then, but now he wondered if those who are truly fey have use of their legs to gambol with Puck and the others. Perhaps, in time, if he were lucky, the fairies would grant him a boon like they had bestowed upon his Aunt Louise.

# A Council of Crows

⚜

The black bird spreads his wings to slow his approach. He extends his talons outward to catch the branch. At the last moment, he flaps three times to stop. He alights on the branch with a practiced skill. Zero airspeed at the precise moment of zero altitude. He bows to the larger bird already perched on the branch.

"It nears time. The old one prepares to depart. We should be there to chant the death song."

The larger bird acknowledges the report as other crows descend upon the branches of the leafless tree. "You have enough to begin. We shall come as soon as the Council sees to our own old one."

The legs of the second bird tense and push. Powerfully, he launches himself from the branch; his wings beat strongly. He propels himself aloft and eastward. As he climbs, he passes others descending toward the Council tree. Among them one whose flight is not so strong as the rest. Whose landing on the branch is not so sure. Feathers more dull than shiny in the slanting autumnal sun, his eyes display a translucent white buildup over the corneas. He is the oldest living member of the flock. He is well respected, and his memories, when shared, have made winter nights seem less long and cold.

The large bird bows to him. "Elder, we have little time, for there is one who has kept to the old ways and expects our help reaching the next realm. Know that we have valued you as a member of our flock, but as it will for all of us, your time has run its appointed course. Now you have become a liability to all of your children and grandchildren, your nieces and nephews. Were the great horned one to take you from the sky, she would be emboldened to try to take others. So too a fox while we forage, or even members of another flock. We will remember you in our song for the old ones, but now you must depart. May your death be painless with no suffering, and may your spirit find itself soaring in the next realm." The chief of the flock bows once more and then thrusts himself into the air. With a thunder of wings, the remainder of the flock follows him. All save the old one, who stays in the tree. He wishes them well as they wing away to the east.

He sits awhile to rest himself, and then he leaves. He does not thrust himself off the branch; rather he falls and extends his wings so that he glides a short distance before he flaps. He does not climb but stays just above the treetops as his path takes him toward the western mountains.

⚜

In the house, the daughter gently touches the old man's face. A loose strand of her hair falls across his forehead. "Dad," she whispers at his ear. "Dad, they are coming."

The old man opens his eyes. He takes a moment to orient himself. The mixture of the pain and the lack of sensory perception, brought on by the injections, make reality and dream difficult to sort one from the other.

He lies in a four-poster bed of sufficient height that he can see westward to the mountains through the windows and French doors. The heavy drapes on all the windows are open and pulled back. The late-afternoon sky is a cold blue. The slanting sun casts long shadows of the leafless oaks and hickories that surround all but the front of the house.

He hears them arriving. The flutter of their wings as they stop their descent, landing in the great white oak tree to the right front of the house. The three crows, there throughout the afternoon, have now become thirty. They walk back and forth on the branches, seeking places out of the wind. They talk among themselves. He listens.

"Perch next to me, yearling," the leader says to a smaller crow. "I will help you sing the song of release."

The smaller crow hops along the branch, stopping next to the leader. He bows, then faces forward, his tail at right angle to the trunk of the great white oak. His sleekness shines like polished black granite. His intelligent dark eyes glisten, coal-like, when struck by the rays of the now-reddening evening sun.

The leader lifts his head, "We begin." He recites:

> Your life has been well lived,
> But now, for you, converging
> Are all realms of time and place.
> Your life and all of history are merging.
> Let go and cast yourself into the space
> That is then, now, and forever.
> Join those who have gone before
> And those who will come after.
> From all we have come,
> And to all we will return.
> Fly away and upward,
> Fly away and upward,
> Ever upward to the realm…

The crows continue skillfully to chant the ancient lay of release. The man understands their song. His hollow-cheeked face forms a smile. Something like the distant memory of light glimmers in his eyes.

⚜

In the kitchen of the house, relatives have gathered to observe the passing of the man.

"I don't understand why we're here. Why didn't he stay in the hospital? We're out here in the middle of nowhere waiting for an old man to die." This from the wife of a grandchild.

"He doesn't want to die in a hospital. He's a deist and a naturalist. As long as I can remember, he's said he wanted to die in his own bed," answers the grandchild's father.

"And the crows. What is all that racket? *Caw! Caw! Caw!* We should all take towels and go out and wave them away from the house so he can die in peace." This from the wife of a great-nephew.

"No!" Again it is the old man's eldest son and the father of the grandchild. He speaks firmly. "The crows have come to help him cross into the next world. It can be a dangerous trip. A soul can lose its way or be snared by a demon. The presence of the crows keeps the demons away. And the crows show the path to the soul of the dying one."

"Where did you learn that crap?" asks the fiftyish nephew, father to the son whose wife wants to scare the crows.

The elder son once again explains. "Suffice it to say my father has lived a long, useful life, and in that life, he learned things about nature and about people that only an astute observer and active participant can learn. He believes man has an innate understanding of nature and of God. He thinks there are basic truths within the natural world that govern how things happen. His understanding is that the more sophisticated man thinks himself, the further he moves away from the natural truths. He believes that myths are based upon an ancient understanding of the natural order, and those myths, at their core, have meaning for man."

The son stops momentarily to sip from the steaming cup of coffee he has been holding, then continues. "Do you think it is a coincidence that my father is dying and we have a flock of crows in the trees outside his bedroom? Do you think those crows could have come to a treeless parking lot outside the hospital? Do you think it unusual that my father has spoken all my life of the legend of the crows and death?"

The questions cause a contemplative but heavy silence in the kitchen. Just as it seems the silence will settle permanently, it is broken by a loud crack from the fireplace as an air pocket in a hickory log finds its way to freedom.

⚜

"Gee, we've been out all afternoon, and we haven't seen a duck yet. I want to use this duck gun Grandfather gave me."

The son and father sit in a duck blind on the edge of the lake in the foothills of the mountains. Their decoys float easily on the mirror-still lake. They have blown their duck calls through their chapped lips, but no ducks have come. The boy fingers the old, long-barreled, single-shot duck gun he received as a birthday present.

"We need to take the boat and bring in the decoys. It will be dark soon." His father looks at the reddish ball descending toward the western mountains.

"Oh, Dad! Come on. Just one shot!" the son pleads.

"What are you going to shoot?" the father asks.

The boy looks around, seeing nothing worthy of the twelve-gauge birdshot, when suddenly a slow-flying crow appears just over the treetops on the eastern edge of the lake. The boy mounts the duck gun, sights down the long barrel, and before his father can stop him, pulls the trigger.

His father's "No!" is far too late. There is an eruption of black feathers as the body of the crow falls off on a wing, spiraling into the water at the edge of the lake.

The father grabs the collar of the retriever to keep him from leaving the blind to fetch the body of the crow.

"We don't shoot crows. It's bad luck." The father is more than perturbed; he is angry. Angry that his son would not remember the rules of hunting he has been taught.

"I'm sorry." The son hangs his head, but only slightly. He is thinking his father should be congratulating him on the shot. He made it at maximum range in the half-light of a failing day. He is too young to care about luck.

⚜

In the bedroom, the eldest son has joined the daughter and the wife. The red of the western sky is reflected on the walls of the bedroom, providing a tone and tint that cause the room to resemble a well-done oil painting with figures in half-tone silhouette.

As the wife holds his hand, the old man smiles once more and closes his eyes.

Outside the crows stop singing. The largest pushes himself off the branch and climbs westward. His flock follows.

⚜

Taking in the decoys, the father, from the corner of his eye, sees two forms climbing upward toward the mountains. Higher and higher they climb. They are unlike any birds he has ever seen. They are of the purest white, like bone just excised from its fleshy cover. He cannot see them straight on, only from the corners of his eyes. His son cannot see them at all when his father attempts to point them out.

Later, the father will publicly doubt what he saw, putting it down to an atmospheric trick of the weak late-autumn sun and the darkening steel-blue sky. But secretly, he will say to himself that he should revisit the tales his grandfather told him. Tales of crows, and death, and souls.

# The Face

⚜

HE WAS NOT BLIND, FOR he could see light. It glowed white, like the sun trying to pierce a thick cloud. He felt almost weightless, as if he were floating in a salt-filled sea. Still, he felt fear. Fear not of where he was, but of not being at all. A fear that this nothing was eternity. Then the face appeared. Someone had leaned over him.

Neither young nor old, the face showed lines from care—but there were laughter lines at the corners of the cloud-gray eyes. Eyes that seemed able to castigate or comfort, almost simultaneously. The dark-brown hair was graying at the temples, and strands of gray streaked the rest of the somewhat-flyaway shock that was not long—but neither was it short. The skin was olive with a bronzed overcast of exposure to the sun. The lips were expressive without being too thin or too full. The otherwise-straight nose was just the least bit crooked at the bridge, but it seemed the perfect nose for the face. The mouth was expressive, and the teeth were white and straight. It was a face that inspired confidence. The face of a friend.

A smile broke the corners of the mouth, and the gray eyes slowly took on the blue of a morning overcoming night. He felt a hand beneath his knees and another beneath his shoulders. He was being lifted up. Up, closer to the face that smiled at him. Closer to the eyes that dispelled the fear of not being. Now he could feel his arm and his hand, and he reached up to touch the face of God.

# About the Author

⚜

Tony Jordan was born in Mobile, Alabama, grew up on the Gulf Coast, and graduated with honors—and a major in religion and theology—from the University of the South in Sewanee, Tennessee. He served as a rescue helicopter pilot in Southeast Asia and later as an instructor, a test pilot, and a squadron commander in the US Air Force. He became a clandestine operations officer with the Central Intelligence Agency in 1979 and earned many of that agency's highest awards over the next twenty-five years. In 2005, he accepted a senior executive position at a major Boston-based technology company.

He now writes from the tower office of his cottage on Spy Hill Farm, in the foothills of the Crab Orchard Mountains of Tennessee, where he is ably supported and appropriately encouraged, when needed, by his wife, Anne, and his BFF, Tailwagger Jack.